The Third Magic

Other books by Welwyn Wilton Katz
Witchery Hill
False Face
(Margaret K. McElderry Books)

Welwyn Wilton Katz

★

THE
THIRD
MAGIC

Margaret K. McElderry Books
NEW YORK

Margaret K. McElderry Books
Macmillan Publishing Company
866 Third Avenue,
New York, NY 10022

Printed in Canada
First United States Edition 1989
10 9 8 7 6 5 4 3 2 1

Library of Congress Cataloging-in-Publication Data
Katz, Welwyn Wilton.
    The third magic.
    Summary: In this interpretation of the Arthurian legend, fifteen-year-old Morgan Lefevre is mistaken for one of her ancestors while visiting England, summoned to the alien world of Nwm, and caught between the opposing cruelties of the two Magics.
    [1. Fantasy] I. Title
PZ7.K15746Th 1989   [Fic]   88-8387
ISBN 0-689-50480-2

*To Stan Dragland, for his help,
encouragement, friendship, and vision;*

*To Shelley Tanaka, for far more
than her wonderful editing;*

*To my brother, Robert Wilton,
for his love of fantasy;*

*And to Albert, for so much it
would take a book to say it.*

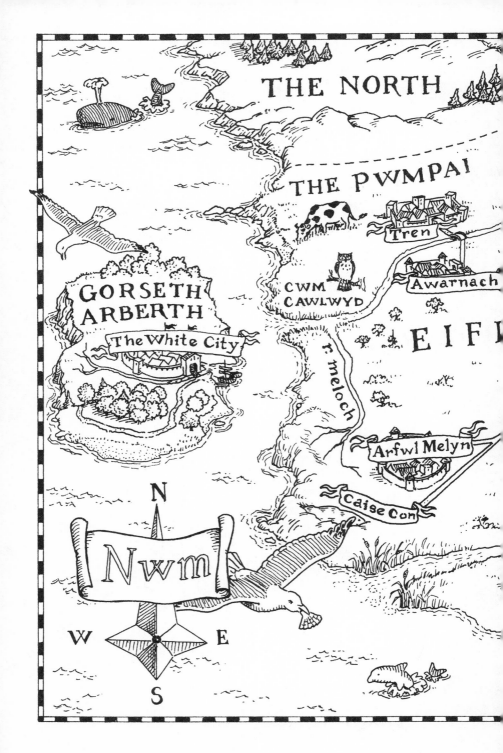

Acknowledgments

I want to express my sincere appreciation to the Canada Council for the financial support which helped make this book possible. I also want to thank my dear friends, Jean Little, Kinny Kreiswirth, Joan Finnegan, Barbara Novak, and Lynda Usprich, who saw me through the logical torments of this book, and gave me the courage to keep going. Special thanks to my mother, Anne Wilton, for sharing, supporting, and caring — and for her macaroni and cheese suppers!

The epigrams at the beginning of each chapter were taken from *The Four Ancient Books of Wales, Containing the Cymric Poems Attributed to the Bards of the Sixth Century,* by William F. Skene (Edmonston and Douglas, Edinburgh, 1868). Translations therein were by the Rev. Robert Williams (1810–1881) and the Rev. D. Silvan Evans (1818–1903).

PART I

ONE

Everyone must give up what he loves.
— Red Book of Hergest I
(A Dialogue Between Myrdin
and his Sister Gwendydd)

O N the island of Gorseth Arberth winter was ending. Some patches of snow remained in the greening woods, but the wind was warm and smelled of woodbine. Earwigs wriggled on the damp moss, and hares scented spring and abandoned their earthy tunnels. On an animal path in the west of the island, sunlight made a heady golden line, almost too straight for nature. A boy strode along it, enjoying the warmth on his shoulders, though he knew he should not. His island name was A'Casta. He called himself Arddu.

His hemp sandals were quiet on the soft earth. He was tall and thin, but despite the bulky sack of herbs on his shoulder, he moved quickly. He had fine, pale hair, and his wide-set eyes were as luminous as moonlight on snow. His face had a shuttered look. His hood had blown back, but he was warm from hurrying and hadn't replaced it.

"Go ahead and stare," he said to a rabbit regarding him from beside the path. The rabbit flicked an ear but did not run away. On Gorseth Arberth man was not something animals feared.

Whenever the trees thinned enough for a clear view, Arddu would look at the sky. It was the brilliant blue of a Linesman's gaze, completely free of clouds. There was only the moon to rest the eyes on, whirling its tiny circle over the island in the midst of that blue dazzle.

Gods, Arddu thought, how the Circle must be hating this!

10

Through all the ages there had been no direct sunlight on the island. But now every morning the great red sun rose bright and clear, and sometimes it was almost evening before clouds covered it up till another dawn. No one on Gorseth Arberth ever talked about it. But even the servients knew it was a sign that the Line's Second Magic was growing, and that the Circle's First Magic was less.

Sooner or later, the Circle would have to do something. Arddu remembered a recent wariness in his sister Rigan's eyes. She was shielding herself a lot these days. He wondered if that meant the Circle was doing something already.

He shook the thought aside. The Circle's plans for the Line were no concern of his. He had a work-shift waiting for him at sunfall, and little time between now and then to get to it.

The sun was high in the sky, and Arddu had not eaten since dawn. He pulled some marroot from his belt pouch, careful not to touch the hellebore juice that had leaked through the sack onto his cloak. Hellebore was a rare herb, but he had found a large stand of it last spring in a forest at the far west of the island. Today he had gone back to collect some for Rigan. Herb lore was one of the things his sister taught him, when she had the time, and the patience.

Today he had used the sack to protect his hands from the juicy stems as he cut them. The last time, when he hadn't done this, his hands had pained and itched for days. Rigan had been unsympathetic. "I warned you hellebore was dangerous," she'd told him.

"I thought you meant to eat," he had protested.

"You'd have died if you had eaten it," she had answered him coolly, shaping poultices of healing yarrow for his palms. "You'll never forget that now, will you?"

Crunching the nourishing marroot as he walked along, he thought about Rigan. She was his twin, born first by only a few minutes, but even after fifteen years of knowing her he did not understand that combination of caring and disdain.

At midafternoon he knelt to drink at one of the many streams that threaded the island. The water was cold. Clouds were rolling in from the west, covering the sun at last. Chilled, Arddu pulled his hood back on. The trail he was following had lost itself in a maze of smaller paths, and the going was slow. When he came to a broader track that wound across the island from one of the southwest villages, he took it, though he usually avoided the well-traveled routes. The White City was still an hour ahead.

A cuckoo called, soft and insinuating. The silence afterward gave it away, an unnatural stillness in which the bird call echoed. Arddu stopped walking. The cuckoo was a Circle bird. When it called like that, Sisters of the First Magic were always nearby.

Arddu hated any encounter with the Circle. He hated the way its Sisters eyed him and never spoke. He would stare in return into their moonlight eyes, their white and haughty faces framed in the corn-silk hair that was as much a sign of First Magic as darkness and blue eyes were a sign of Second, and to him and to them it was like looking into a distorted mirror.

He was male. He was without magic. Yet he had the skin and eyes and hair of First Magic. Could the Sisters of the Circle be blamed for naming him A'Casta, Abomination?

Every chance he could, he avoided them. He had learned the art of disappearing, even though his gray cloak and leggings branded him. No one else on the world of Nwm wore gray. The Sisters of the Circle wore stark black and icy silver; the men of the Line a flaunting scarlet and gold. The servients, whether they served the Circle or the Line, wore a brown as dull and downtrodden as the earth they walked on.

The gray clothing had been Rigan's doing. *My brother is no servient*, she had declared haughtily. She had been four years old, a mere child. But the Circle had listened to her, as it always listened to one of its own.

Rigan wore silver and black. She was his twin, and he loved her as he loved nothing else, but Rigan was a Sister of the First Magic.

Cw-cw, cw-cw. The cuckoo was just ahead of him, round a bend hidden by larches. Arddu tilted his head to listen. He heard the crunch of footsteps and the murmur of female voices. Sisters; at least two of them. He headed quickly for a grove of beeches. Two Sisters would be bad enough. More would make a Circle, and such a joining did not happen without purpose.

Arddu dropped his sack into a hollow, then sat down between two of the trees, hunching his knees to his forehead. He sat very still, a gray shadow among other gray shadows, not looking up.

The Sisters came closer. They were on the main track, but moving very slowly. Two only, Arddu decided, deciphering the sounds. One walked with dragging footsteps: an old one, unusual this far from the city.

"Would you rest a little, Dreamer? There is a log over there, near those beeches."

Rigan's voice! Arddu groaned silently. Rigan, by all the gods, inviting another Sister to sit not a stone's throw away from her own twin brother — and that other Sister the Dreamer, who rarely set foot on the island at all! Circle business, this must be, Circle business with a vengeance. Rigan would be furious if she discovered him. He tucked his chin deeper into his chest and tried not to breathe.

"We will both sit," the Dreamer said. "I have been too long on board *Kynthelig*. It seems I have forgotten how to walk." Her voice wasn't what Arddu expected from someone old. It was strong and crackling as winter's hardest frost.

A twig snapped. The footsteps came closer. Arddu heard a rustle of cloth as they sat down. "For someone who has forgotten how to walk, you have managed a fair distance," Rigan pointed out.

"And for someone who has just been given a Made Magic, *you* have managed a fair silence."

Defensively, Rigan said, "You would have told me anything the Dream permitted."

"All hidden knowledge weakens First Magic," the Dreamer replied coldly. "Unity is what makes the Circle strong."

"In that case you need not have waited for my questions."

Arddu blanched at the silence that followed Rigan's words. "Very well," his sister said, her tone more conciliatory, "why *did* you give me the jade circlet?"

"You are to carry it until it must be used."

"Used by me?"

The world seemed to darken. The Dreamer's voice went low and chanting. "There is a world; I see it. I see days of no moon. I see a circle broken; I see the two-ended line curved. It will cost much, Morrigan. You will suffer with it."

Rigan cleared her throat. "I ask again. I am to use it?"

"Not unless there is no other way. It is — I think — not entirely yours."

"It is for use on my missioning, not on Nwm?"

Missioning? Arddu stiffened. Rigan sent to another world, away from Nwm, away from him? Other Sisters might be missioned, sent to use their wits and their magic to Encircle the known Nwm-like worlds. But not Rigan, not his twin! Rigan could not have kept something as important as this a secret from him!

"The jade circlet goes with you to Earth," the Dreamer affirmed. "But only the Mother knows where it will be used."

"After I leave," Rigan said, "what will happen to — Arddu?"

"The A'Casta has his own Dream."

Footsteps, one set dragging, the other as light as Arddu's own. "He does not know I am leaving," Rigan persisted. "May I tell him? It is tonight, after all."

Tonight! The blood pounded in Arddu's ears. Rigan was leaving tonight!

"Only you can determine what the A'Casta should be told." Even at a distance the Dreamer's voice cut with its coldness.

"Let him stay on the island, Dreamer. He is no danger to anyone. And he is my brother."

"On Earth," the Dreamer said, "you will have a new brother."

Arddu thought he would be sick. When he tried to listen again, even the rustle of their movements was gone. He waited for a long time. Then, leaving the sack of herbs where it lay, he got stiffly to his feet. Somehow he found the trail again. The beeches loomed behind him. Shadows lay thick on the larchwood. Arddu checked himself over, seeking out the flint knife at his ankle, the pack of marroot on his hip. He had no water-pouch with him, no fishnet. He would need both, if they let him live.

He saw no one the whole way to the city. Even there, few people were about. It was the quiet time before the shift change, when those not on duty were still asleep. In his tiny room in the sleeping hall he collected his gear. Then he took off his cloak and carried it into the next room.

It was a wedge-shaped nook identical to his own, except that there were two beds in it, not one. The boy Drw was asleep in one of them. Drw didn't seem to care that he himself was only a servient. He didn't even mind Arddu's looks. The two boys fished together when their schedules permitted. Drw was the closest thing to a friend that Arddu had.

Arddu looked at Drw's tired face, and decided not to wake him. From a wooden hook beside the bed he took the other boy's old brown cloak, leaving his own in its place. Drw wouldn't wear it, but it would give him something to exchange for a new brown one. And Arddu had to have something ordinary to cover his face and hair, if they let him leave the island.

And if they didn't let him leave? If they killed him instead? He shrugged. What would it matter then what he was wearing? He slipped the brown cloak on, feeling its roughness. Then he left Drw sleeping, and went away.

★

He walked for a long time. When the sun began to set he found himself beside the sea. It was silent today, foaming and bubbling in stony whirlpools that imitated the moon. Away from the birchwood, away from the Nine Rivers and the White City, away from the fertile green, the island was stark, with rocky outcroppings piercing the bleached sands. Seabirds, white on white, haunted the misty skies, mewing at the ever-circling moon. To Arddu this sea-licked beach was the truth about the island, the wintry core of all that was First Magic. It was the bare bones that lay beneath all that green and fleshy magic farther inland.

While Arddu had wandered, Rigan had finally told him about her missioning. She had done it from a distance, using the mindspeech. The ability to communicate mentally was something Arddu and Rigan had shared since their twin birth. From the start they had used the mindspeech only with the other's consent, but now and then Arddu overheard more of Rigan's thoughts than she intended. This was one of those times. All the while Rigan's mind was informing him about her missioning to Earth, he was hearing her awareness that she should have told him sooner, that she shouldn't be telling him like this at all. It was only because of that hidden shame of hers that he was waiting to meet her now.

With a long, straight stick he sketched a spiral in the sand. It was an idle act at first, but as time went by he concentrated on it until it seemed to take on meaning, though he didn't understand it. He stayed in the center, turning with his spiral, south to the empty ocean; east to the Pwmpai and the burning lands beyond; north to chaos, heart-lurching, unknowable; then west again, west to the heart of his own lush island.

I don't know anywhere but here, he thought. I can't even get away, not on my own.

Numbly, his stick continued moving. Ships often left Gorseth Arberth; fishing ships, mostly, some island traders. Now and then he himself had gone with them. But today there were no ordinary ships, not for him. The fishing docks were empty, and no servient there would look at him.

They know, Arddu thought. Somehow, they've found out.

Behind him, he heard Rigan.

"My Sisters are going to banish you," she said. She spoke aloud. Her voice was harsh with control. "They have promised not to kill you."

He said nothing, not even with his mind. His spiral was wider now, his stick pointing east to the lands of the Line.

"You knew I might be missioned one day. Arddu, there isn't anything I can do!"

He looked at her then. Her face was calmer than her eyes. "I'm a Sister first," she said.

"You're my sister, too, Rigan."

"Now I am your sister. But before the sun rises I will be born again on another world. I will be an infant again — I will have a mother —"

"*We* had a mother, once!"

She made an impatient movement. "All my training has been for this mission, Arddu. I was born for it. Even my name is what it is because of a history that must take place."

"What about me? I was born with you, Rigan."

"An accident of mating! By the Mother, Arddu, would you have me nursemaid you forever?"

He turned away from her. There was a long silence. Slowly, then, her hand went to his shoulder and turned him around. "I'm sorry," she said. "I don't want you hurt. But I must perform this missioning."

"Will we be together once it is done?"

Her eyes silvered over, and he knew the answer."

I'll never see you again. He used the mindspeech, the grief arrowing from his mind into hers.

She answered him aloud. "Things could never be the same between us, even if you weren't banished. Time runs strangely between worlds. On Earth I may live half a lifetime while only a few hours go by here. When I am finally summoned back to Nwm my mind will be older than you can ever be."

Take me with you!

"You will be my past." Hard as stone. Still speaking aloud, denying his mindspeech, denying him.

He refused to accept it. *You could take me, if you wanted. A Mind-Meld — it'd be easy, Rigan, we're so close —*

Not that close! Mindspeech at last. Grateful for that much, he tried to shrug off the meaning, but she was going on. *Even if I could do it, your body here would die. You would be permanently a part of me. You would have no identity of your own, no friends. But you would have enemies. You cannot imagine such enemies, Arddu!*

A vision then, a bearded face with flaring eyes, a scarlet and gold cloak, a firepot burning. It was a Linesman. Arddu wanted to respond, but she wouldn't let him. Like winter in his mind she went on.

The M'rlendd is the fifth most powerful Linesman on all Nwm. Am I to face him on a hostile world like Earth with none of my Sisters to aid me, and your lack of magic always there hindering me?

His stick dragged sand, heavy as clay. South, east, north, west; and no place to go, nowhere on all of Nwm. He faced her.

You talk about hostile worlds! What about here? First Magic's failing fast, and Second is growing. The Circle's planning something, not on some godsforsaken outworld like Earth, but here on Nwm. You're leaving me on a world that's at the edge of disaster, and you don't even care!

How do you know about the Circle's plans? her mind stabbed. She was wide open to him. In her thoughts Arddu saw a ship, dark as a bird under the moon, and on board that ship he saw three of Rigan's Sisters and knew their names. Gwyar, Elphin, and Heledd, three whose task was to begin a war.

War! Stunned, he saw it in Rigan's mind, the Circle and the Line battling one another over all Nwm, towns burning and the sea rising and Nwm a changed world forever and forever.

And then Rigan slammed up her shield and the vision was gone, and suddenly she was probing his mind.

Betrayed, Arddu gaped at her. The mindprobe was something the Circle did. Rigan had never done it to him before. It hurt, and it shamed him; for a moment he almost hated her. Somehow he locked away the vision he had seen in her mind behind a shield he'd never known he had. His eyes were like glittering mirrors.

When it was over, he said scornfully, "And if I had known the Circle's so important plans, what would you have done to me?"

"You didn't," Rigan said, "so it doesn't matter, does it?"

Arddu turned his back. Behind that newly discovered shield his mind wept.

"They're sending *Kynthelig* for you," she said then.

The *Kynthelig* was no ordinary ship. Sailing strictly by the Dreamer's dream, it was the only ship on all Nwm that could take outsiders to and from Gorseth Arberth. Arddu tried to imagine himself a passenger on that ship, an outsider for now and forever. His throat shut tight at the thought.

She tried again. "Where will you go?"

He only looked out over the leaden sea.

"This is not easy for me, either," she said then, the closest to a plea he had ever heard her make.

He struggled with himself, but could not face her. "Good-bye, *Morrigan*." Willing her to go. Unable to bear it if it had to be he, first.

She had always understood him, when she wanted. He felt her fingers on his cheek, lingering tentatively, as if aware for the first time that they might not be welcome. Then, with a swish of her black-and-silver cloak, she went away.

TWO

Not of mother and father,
When I was made, did my Creator create me.
Of nine-formed faculties,
Of the fruit of fruits,
Of the fruit of the primordial God.
— Book of Taliessin VIII
(The Battle of Godeu)

THE door was featureless and bare, unpainted, smelling faintly of apples. A burglar would have scoffed at the simple lock. There ought to have been a number on the door, but no one had bothered. The attic room, they called it. There was only one.

Hesitating in front of the door, Morgan Lefevre gripped the old jade horseshoe in her pocket. It wasn't exactly a horseshoe, more like a circle broken in half, but Morgan's grandmother had called it that when she gave it to her, and so Morgan did as well. "It's only lucky for girls," Grandma had said. "I got it from my mother, and she from hers. If I'd had a daughter instead of your father, the horseshoe would have gone to her."

Dad would have liked to own the horseshoe, Morgan knew. He loved old things, especially when they had come down his family line. But he didn't need a lucky charm. He was like a magnet, the way good things just seemed to come to him.

"Well, Rapunzel," he said now, from the stairs behind her, "how do you like your tower?"

Morgan looked at him uncertainly. Dad was the host of a television series about history called *Human Nature*, and to

20

Morgan he was always the TV host, even at home, even with her. Other people loved his joking and his charm, and sometimes, wistfully, Morgan did, too. But she never knew how to respond. Even if she had known, joking back would have made her feel too much like one of his fans.

Dad had dropped her suitcase on the third-floor landing, and was eyeing her keenly. "You're moving pretty slowly, for a girl who couldn't wait to get here."

Startled, Morgan blinked at him. The whole time the TV crew had been filming its way through England, he'd been engrossed in his work, seeming too busy to pay attention to anything else. How had he known she was only marking time till they could get to Tintagel?

Tintagel. She had read and reread the legends. Here, once, had been the mightiest castle in Cornwall, so strong that its walls could be breached only by trickery. Here a queen had betrayed her husband and given up her child to a sorcerer. Here, hundreds and hundreds of years ago, King Arthur had been born. It didn't matter that Dad had said the castle hadn't even been built when the real King Arthur was alive. To Morgan the very name Tintagel breathed magic.

The way here had done nothing to dispel that magic. The lowering sky, the coast road with the sea sighing against the rocks below, the salt wind, the gray inn perched on a crag across the cove from the ruins of Tintagel — all of it was exactly right. Now just her room remained to be discovered, and Tintagel itself.

Morgan formed relationships with places; with things, too. The green jade horseshoe was one. She didn't know why she loved it so much, any more than she knew why sometimes she hated things on sight. When her father was getting ready for this program on the Celts of ancient Britain, he had brought home an iron necklet that he called a torc. Morgan had grown sick and pale and refused so vehemently even to touch it that Mom had wanted to take her temperature. "I thought she would love it," she had heard her father protest to Judith Lefevre later. And then Mom had snapped out something about how both he and Morgan spent too much time thinking, and Morgan had heard no more.

"Apple wood, I think," Dad said now, his vivid blue eyes twinkling.

"What?" Morgan said, bewildered.

"The door. The way you've been staring at it, I thought you must be trying to identify its molecules."

"Oh." She flushed a little.

"Don't you want to see your room?"

Without answering, she shoved the key into the ancient lock and pushed the door open. At once the room reached out to her. Cool, open, bare, windy — she blinked. No, that wasn't the room, it was the headland outside, wide to the sea with empty, spray-damped stone. She could see it through the window that made up the whole of one wall. It was a huge, screenless piece of glass with side panels that cranked out. They had been left open, letting in sound and smell and light, so that the room seemed continuous with the outside. A seabird mewed, wild and free. It might have been in the room.

Morgan stood very still, lost in the wonder of it. Sun and clouds, rock and sea. . . . At night, when she slept, she would taste the salt on the wind, and the moon's half-light would surround her.

"In Caer Pedryvan, in the isle of the strong door,
The twilight and pitchy darkness were mixed together."

Her father was quoting the strange words softly, making them sound beautiful and lonely and fitting to this special room. Morgan looked at him, dismayed by his understanding.

"It's from *The Spoils of Annwm*," he explained, misunderstanding her frown, "an old Celtic poem about King Arthur's journeys in the Underworld." His voice became brisk. "Some old bard must have been pretty desperate for a story, don't you think?" He went over to the window. "Hey, you can see the castle from here." He was leaning out of the left window, dark hair whipping in the wind. She told herself there was no room for her.

"Even in ruins it gives you the shivers," he said, half to himself. "But Judas Priest, that path! How they'll get the cameras up there, I don't know."

Human Nature was John Lefevre's series, though the Canadian Broadcasting Corporation paid for it. He always knew the kind of show that would work. People called him a magician. The truth, he said, was that he was a combination of romantic and shark, and Canadians were fascinated by both. Morgan's mother always smiled when he said that. She never told anyone about the closed study door at home, his days in the library, the endless meetings for which she provided coffee and silence.

Morgan got angry, sometimes, when she saw Judith Lefevre cleaning up after one of these research sessions, or when her father joked to the writers how Judy could get more cups of coffee per pound than anyone he knew. Judith always smiled, though Morgan could never understand how. Obviously Mom didn't care what any of them thought. She didn't care about their beloved history, either. She always said that the people she was interested in were alive, not dead. She was not the kind of person you needed to be protective about, but somehow, Morgan always was.

Dad was smiling at her. "Don't you want to see Tintagel?"

"Yes. Sure."

But she made no move toward the window. She wrapped her arms around herself as if she were cold.

"This room gets quite a breeze," Dad said. "Do you want me to shut the window?"

"I like the wind."

He smiled. "I like it, too. As a matter of fact, I like pretty well everything about this place."

"It is nice," Morgan agreed, a little shyly.

"We Celts know a good thing when we see one, huh?" He smiled companionably. "Though the climate — well, I wouldn't mind some more sun, myself, but even your mother admits England is a lovely green, and you can't have that without a little rain!"

"I guess I'd better get unpacked," Morgan said.

His smile faded. "I should check about sending that videotape to Toronto, anyway. Then maybe I'll take a walk." He headed for the door.

Feeling unaccountably guilty, she called after him, "Thanks for carrying my suitcase up, Dad."

"Sure," he said, and was gone.

For a while Morgan stayed away from the window. There was an old trunk in the corner of the room near the door, and she made herself examine it, but the great gusty window at her back wouldn't let her alone. She wanted to go to it, she wanted to look out, to lean out as her father had done, to see to the limits of rock and sky and sea, out to that little edge of Cornwall where King Arthur had been born. The strength of her wanting frightened her, and she turned instead to her suitcase with its neat piles of clothing. But the whole time she unpacked, the window seemed to be commanding her. Finally, unable to bear it any longer, she let herself obey. She went over to the window and leaned out, and her long hair was caught by the wind and streamed like pale seaweed in front of her face. Through it, at last, she looked at Tintagel.

And she saw ruins, and knew them: a monastery's ruins, not a castle's; not at all the same ruins her father had seen.

And she saw a path, steep and wild, but it was not the one the cameramen would hate, fifteen hundred years later.

And she saw a walled garden, there at the top of the world with the sea crashing below, and there were no plants in that garden, only dead soil, and the marks of a great burning.

And she saw a man in the center, staring into a firepot; a scarlet and gold man, cavernously lean. He turned and looked at her, at Morgan on the path below him; and though she was not alone, though another came with her and held her hand and jerked impatiently when she would not move, still there seemed to be only Morgan and that man.

The M'rlendd, she thought. Her enemy.

★

She ought to have hated the window after that, and the room with it, but she didn't. At first she didn't even try to deny it. She merely accepted it: a vivid flash from another world, a world where she herself belonged. It didn't last long, only an instant, really, but in that instant she was another Morgan with other eyes, seeing a Tintagel from a long-dead age.

24

And then her mother came in. "No screens here, either," she said. There was something else, something about dinner, but her voice sounded fuzzy, as if from a great distance. When Morgan didn't turn away from the window, she came over and touched her hand. "Gooseflesh," she said. "You should get some more clothes on, honey. What're you looking at, anyway?"

"Just the view," Morgan muttered, pulling herself back from the abyss.

It had not been real, she told herself. She was Morgan Lefevre, not that other girl; she lived in the twentieth century; Tintagel was a ruined castle, nothing more. She had no enemies, and even if she had, it would not be that man whose face, peering out from a scarlet hood, shone iron-hard and grim.

Her mother looked briefly out the window. "Personally, I'm getting sick of views. You all unpacked?"

Not real, Morgan told herself again. *Not.* Her mother was waiting. What had she asked?

"Are you okay?" Judith Lefevre asked in concern. "You're cold as ice, and your lips are almost blue."

"I'm fine," Morgan said, pulling herself together.

"You're tired out. You've been up reading half the night every single night since we left Toronto. And having nightmares when you do sleep, probably, with the kind of thing you read. Sorcerers and swords and people disemboweling each other all over the place! No wonder you're such a bad color!"

"I'm not. Or, anyway, not because I've been staying up reading."

"You don't think you're getting sick, do you?"

Suddenly Morgan longed to tell her. Mom would laugh and say it was just a daydream. She'd make it so unreal that Morgan would never have to think about it again.

The image returned, that iron face in its scarlet hood, those blue eyes wide and merciless as a desert sky. You could start a fire with those eyes, Morgan thought. She shivered.

Her mother was watching her and frowning. "I'm not sick," Morgan muttered. "Maybe I am just tired."

"It's bad enough your father spending all his spare time reading," Judith said, rubbing her forehead with her thin white fingers. "But you, Morgan! Fifteen years old and buried in the past, Arthur and Lancelot and God knows who else. A bunch of nonsense, all of it —"

"I'll go to bed early tonight," Morgan said quickly. "I won't read anything. Nothing at all. I promise."

She was always making promises to her mother. She always meant the promises, and she always tried her hardest to keep them. Because Morgan loved her mother. To make Mom happy, Morgan would have promised almost anything, even if she failed in the end.

"No shining swords? Not even one legend about Avalon?" Judith asked, not quite smiling. "How will you manage without your daily dose of King Arthur?"

"I'm not that interested in him. I just hate looking dumb. Everybody here keeps talking about him —"

"Ego." Her mother shook her head. "Historical experts showing off to each other. There's no point trying to impress people like that. They don't expect us to have brains, anyway. They know we're only here to pretty up Dad's show."

There were to be some family shots in this particular episode of *Human Nature*, the CBC having decided that the Canadian public wanted to know what the Lefevres were like. "Ruin my image," John had said; but joking or not, Judith and Morgan had come.

It was an eye-opener to Morgan, being with her father day after day, seeing him at work. At home he was detached, friendly enough, but mostly on his way in or out. But here! "Wildfire-time," someone had groaned in Winchester, when John was first shown the so-called Round Table of King Arthur; and Morgan had understood at once. Her father had devoured every fact and figure he could get his hands on, whole forests of them, truth and legend alike. Then, while other people were still reeling, he abandoned almost everything, leaving only what he called the important bits, already branded with the John Lefevre stamp. Blazing with enthusiasm, infecting everyone with one idea and then going on to something new, leaving other people half-consumed behind him — it was exhausting to watch, so much so that only afterward would Morgan realize how wonderful it had been.

She was unable to keep herself from talking about it, but her mother only raised her brows. "You weren't quite such a fan last Awards Day," she said coolly. Morgan went silent, remembering how her father hadn't seen her take three of her grade's subject prizes. He'd said he was coming, but there had been a crisis at the studio. At least Mom had been at the presentation. She didn't care all that much about high marks, but she cared a great deal about Morgan.

"Better get some long pants on, sweetie," she was saying now. "Those shorts are definitely not designed for an evening in Cornwall."

Morgan grimaced. "I'll bet those boring old Celts of Dad's went around naked."

That made her mother smile. Sucking up, Morgan told herself, and, remembering the way her father had recited that poem, was suddenly ashamed.

The moment the door closed behind her mother, Morgan's window came to life again. She felt it even without looking, a lurch of her stomach that was only half fear. Slowly she turned to face it.

There it was, a window, that was all, yet unmistakably, it called to her. There was no way to ignore it. She tried, huddling back into the corner by the trunk, her arms wrapped protectively around her chest. But she simply couldn't stay there. Gnawing at her lip, she headed for the clothing spread out on her bed. She would get changed and go for a walk before dinner. She would find the lounge and watch some TV. She wouldn't — she *would not* — go over to that window again.

But somehow, she was already there.

Without looking out the window, she took her belt off and buckled the ornate iron part around her wrist. She didn't reason it through, she merely did it. Something inside her protested, but she didn't listen, not even when the buckle burned, cold as fear against her skin. Still looking only at her belt, she tied its other end to the crank-handle of the window.

Then, tethered by iron, she leaned out, and looked again toward Tintagel.

And she saw a roofless, ruined castle.

And she saw a steep path that the cameramen would hate.

And she saw, at the top, a flat, empty, gardenless plateau where only her father walked.

THREE

Fly thee hence and hide thyself...
Prostration is useless, thy creeping will cause a noise.
— Red Book of Hergest XVI

IT was very late. Arddu had not slept and had not eaten. Rigan was gone. He had felt it happen, felt the pattern that was his sister dissolving, her essence sent across time to a world he could never know. Emotion had left him empty, a husk. Now and then he looked at the sandy spiral he had made, glittering in the moonlight.

The sea was quiet, barely moving. The image of the moon swept through it, a watery circle lighting blackness to silver. Arddu rubbed his eyes. There was a dinghy out there. Now he could see the black and silver shape of the Dreamer rowing. Her back was to him. The clean swish of water as her oars dipped, the clear tinkle of droplets as she brought them forward again, were the only sounds in all the ivory night.

Arddu had met the Dreamer only once in his life before today. She hadn't been Dreamer then, only Llwch Llawynnog, come to the northern Pwmpai with two of her Sisters to perform the infant testing. In the years since that day he had often tried to imagine it, his mother's mute despair as she opened the door to the three who had come, the Sisters' shock on discovering that one of this servient woman's white-haired, pale-eyed babies was a male. And then the part he didn't have to imagine because it had happened too many times since: the vice of First Magic squeezing what he was out of him, and finding that he had no magic.

Why, after the testing, had the three Sisters taken him to their own island? Rigan was First Magic; he understood their taking her. But why him? Why hadn't they merely killed him as they had his mother? Rigan had never explained. "All I know is that it had something to do with Llwch Llawynnog becoming Dreamer," she had told him.

"She became Dreamer at our testing? Why? Was it because of us?"

"The dream needed a voice, and Ysmere's wasn't there." Ysmere had been the Circle's previous Dreamer.

"What happened to Ysmere?" he had asked.

"She — went north."

And then, no matter how he had pressed her, she would say no more.

Swish, drip, swish, drip. Effortlessly the Dreamer came toward him. She didn't look over her shoulder to check where he was. She didn't gesture when it was time for him to come. But he knew. He got to his feet, then wrapped his brown cloak around his chest and waded out to her, to Llwch Llawynnog who had helped to kill his mother.

She said nothing when he climbed into the bow. Her back was still toward him. He watched it for a while, too numb to make the effort not to. She maneuvered the dinghy around, then began those steady, tireless strokes again. *Swish, drip, swish, drip.* He got up the energy to turn the other way. A long distance offshore the ship *Kynthelig* rode the swell like a silver bird, tugging at its anchor. The wind was freshening. Arddu didn't look back. At last they were at the *Kynthelig*'s side. Without prompting he made the climb up the rope ladder.

Only once did he meet the Dreamer's eyes. She was hoisting the anchor, and he got in the way. For an endless moment they stared at each other. Then, heart pounding, he got right away from her. He had expected to see hatred in her eyes, or maybe indifference. He hadn't expected to see fear.

Huddling into his cloak in the bow of the ship, the wind blowing spray into his face like sleety tears, he stared into the east. And the *Kynthelig*'s sails billowed and the ancient wooden timbers groaned and the water foamed around the ship's keel, and all the while the rolling horizon brightened with the approach of dawn.

★

On the shore a boy's lithe brown figure ran to the water's edge, watching the moonlit dot that was the *Kynthelig* vanish into the east. Drw was alone. He had made very sure there were no witnesses. Nevertheless, he waited until the ship was completely out of sight. Then he flipped back his cloak. On his left arm was a hooded falcon, linked to his wrist by a fine iron chain. Keeping the bird's hood on, he pressed the falcon's head to his own temple.

"The Morrigan has been missioned," he whispered. "The A'Casta is banished."

The bird had carried other messages to the Line, but none had been received as this one would be. Drw slipped off the bird's hood and released the chain. The bird's bright eyes gleamed at him, intelligent and disdainful.

"Go!" Drw snapped. Like the crack of a whip it flew off into the east. Drw watched, his face twisted. "So now you've got what you wanted," he told the eastern sky. "You don't need me anymore."

But they wouldn't let him go. Somewhere in the east there was a man who had once been Drw's father. For years now the Linesmen had owned him. Now they owned Drw, too.

And Circle or Line, Drw thought bitterly, once either of them owned you, they owned you forever.

★

Dawn came at last. Arddu squinted into it, then lowered his eyes to a hump of land rising whalelike out of the sea beneath. He recognized Cwm Cawlwyd at the mouth of the River Ffraw. He had been there once before with Drw, brought by the other boy's uncle to catch salmon. Arddu remembered that day: the sun and the moon glittering at each other across the river; the white dunes seeming to stretch forever to the north and south; cormorants stretching black necks into the shimmer; the warning boom of bitterns. In *Kynthelig*'s bow, Arddu relived that memory, while Cwm Cawlwyd grew closer and closer and his own island more and more lost.

The *Kynthelig* shuddered to a stop. The Dreamer moved quickly, stern to bow, anchoring the ship with a netted boulder. Then she hauled a plank from beside the gunwale and stretched it across to a large flat rock on Cwm Cawlwyd. Somehow Arddu made himself climb up to it. The sun had not quite risen. He knew he was expected to go before it did.

Three steps, one after the other. Now he was on Cwm Cawlwyd. The only thing he heard was the scraping sound of the plank being drawn up behind him.

She would not leave until he had chosen his direction. He knew that without being told. He wanted to sit and think, but after all, what was there to think about? North was madness, east beyond the Pwmpai was the Line itself, and west there was only ocean. He had to go south.

He also knew that in the end it would make no difference. On Nwm, there was only the Circle and the Line. If the Circle wouldn't have him, sooner or later the Line would.

And in his mind, endlessly spiraling, was the thought that surely, surely the Circle would know that, too.

★

The day passed. He traveled along the beach until it became a mass of tumbledown cliffs, then headed southeast to easier terrain. This land had some of the black soil of the distant Pwmpai, but farms were fewer and stronger built. Arddu kept well away from them. As night approached, he took shelter in a grove of willows, then ate a fish he had caught earlier on the beach. It tasted like dust, but afterward he felt stronger. While the sun sank he drank from his water pouch, filled at a spring that bubbled up near one of the willows. He could hear dogs barking, a distant sound that made him uneasy.

Automatically he looked up, seeking birds in a flock, Circle birds that might be winging too low, too slow, for nature. But there was only a solitary dot high in the darkening sky. It didn't have the way of flight of an owl. He had half expected the Circle to follow him, but apparently his banishment was complete. Yet the solitary bird disturbed him. It was keeping to one place, hovering directly over him. There was only one bird that did that, watching its prey until it was sure of it.

The bird was a hawk, and he was its prey.

His heart thumped. Stupid, he berated himself. A single hawk in the sky, and already he was imagining himself the Line's prisoner. Why would Second Magic be interested in a brown-cloaked traveler who must seem only a servient? He had kept his hood on; not even a hawk's eyes could have seen his hair. The bird couldn't know he had anything to do with Gorseth Arberth.

As if to prove his point, the hawk suddenly darted off. Arddu scrambled out of his shelter to watch. The hawk was speeding into the east as if pulled by an invisible line. And why not? It was sunset. The bird would be returning to its nest in the hills. But for a long moment Arddu followed that small black dot into the east, into the misty purple horizon where the hills began and the Circle's power ended.

At dawn the hawk was back. It didn't leave Arddu once all day, a high, hovering companion he couldn't lose, no matter how he tried. He went to sleep that night thinking of it, and dreams of it haunted him.

And when he awoke the next day to an iron sword at his throat and men on horses watching him, he wasn't even surprised.

★

They removed his hood first. His hair glittered silver in the morning sun, and his moonlight eyes shone at them. "Circle," growled the one with the sword, and spat.

Two of the riders flinched and made a warding sign with their hands, but the other mounted man only said calmly, "So despite his cloak, he is the A'Casta."

Stunned, Arddu stared at him. A wandering hawk might have become suspicious enough of him to fetch the Line, though Arddu couldn't imagine why. But to know his name — his island name — it was impossible!

The man returned his look professionally. His eyes were not blue, and his cloak was the color of dried blood, more brown than red. He carried a weapon, too, a thing incompatible with Second Magic. Clearly he was no Linesman. Yet his colors showed he was under the Line's orders, one of that group of Line assassins called Red Cloaks. Second Magic needed

33

the Red Cloaks because it didn't have the Circle's ability to dispense death by magic. It had many powers that some thought worse, but not the Spelled Death.

The sword at Arddu's throat pricked deeper. He lifted his chin to it. His eyes took on the bluish sheen of ice in moonlight.

"Chain him, Custennin," their leader ordered roughly.

Too surprised to resist, Arddu let it happen, the cold of iron linking his arms, a blue manacle on each foot. What were they going to do with him? They knew his name. Did that mean they knew his relationship to Rigan as well? Did they think that by kidnapping him they could gain access to her somehow? For the first time, he was grateful she was gone from Nwm.

The leader of the Red Cloaks waited till Arddu was safely shackled, then dismounted, coming so close to Arddu that his meat-eater's breath dilated the boy's nostrils. Keeping his eyes hard and careful on Arddu's face, he searched him, taking away his knife, fishnet, and water pouch, then throwing the hood over his face. Strong arms made a bundle of him, lifting him up and strapping him into a saddle.

A spare horse, Arddu thought. They were that sure of me.

No one spoke. A whip cracked, and the horses leaped forward. Into the wind and the brightening sun they headed, galloping along the pathless lands into the east, into the hands of the Line.

★

"The A'Casta is here, Power-Seeker."

"Bring him, then. But first, meat. You know the kind."

The servient left, running. The man who remained turned back to the window with a swirl of his golden cloak, his blue eyes looking out on the road with a marked lack of satisfaction. His fingers flexed impatiently against the window frame, then jerked up to his torc, a broken golden circle glittering against the tan of his neck. Menw Power-Seeker, second in Line only to the Sdhe, was not a man to enjoy waiting. Yet he had chosen to be here, waiting in this hovel in gods-rotting Arfwl Melyn. He was second in Line, but he wanted to be first.

34

Running footsteps returned. Menw smelled meat. He turned to examine it. The small carcase was fully identifiable. He tore off a limb, casually, then decided to wait to eat it till the boy was brought. They ate no red meat, those Circle-spawn. They certainly ate no red meat of *this* kind.

"Would you see the prisoner now, Power-Seeker?"

Menw jerked his head, and the servient backed away, opening the door behind him without turning around. A Red Cloak came in, then two more. Between them, clanking in the iron chains that bound him, was a brown-cloaked boy. He looked at Menw, at the red-juiced limb in his hand, and he vomited.

Menw waited till he was finished. Then he took a bite of meat. "Now then, boy," he said, chewing and chewing, "I want you to tell me everything you know of the Circle's new scheme to destroy us."

★

It lasted almost a day. Many times Arddu tried to die. It was not allowed. Second Magic entered his mind, and he was a book to be read. No pettiness in him was left unknown, nothing good remained unsullied. Rigan, too. All that she was to him, the love and the uncertainty, the striving to please, the loneliness when she was away from him, the loneliness when she was there.

"She is your sister. She tells you things. What did she tell you, boy? What?"

The Linesman did not wound. There would be no visible scars. But in the end he knew. The warlike vision Arddu had caught from his sister in their final meeting was ripped out and laid before the man like a corpse.

"A world in chaos," Menw said. "The sisters Gwyar, Elphin, and Heledd sent to start an out-and-out war. That is all she told you?" He was drenched in sweat. "Gods burn you, boy, no specifics?"

Arddu's silver eyes blinked, the blindness in them fading. "She didn't tell me."

"The Circle attempting something so new and dangerous it could end the world of Nwm forever. And your sister, your

35

twin, abandoning you to that fate without even telling you what it is?"

A Sister first. Always a Sister first. "She didn't tell me," Arddu repeated dully.

"A pity for both of us she didn't." His torc slid on his neck. "It'll be even more of a pity for your beloved Rigan."

Bile rose in Arddu's mouth. "What — what do you mean?"

"I mean your pattern, boy. Your bloodline. We know how like the Morrigan you are. The Sdhe intends to use that. We're going to suck the pattern out of you, A'Casta, and then we are going to use it to summon your sister from Earth."

Arrdu's eyes turned leaden. "You can't!" He was almost choking.

"What is missioned can be summoned," Menw said. "All we need is the pattern."

"But Second Magic can't summon First!"

"What does someone like you know of magic?"

Arddu could scarcely get the words out. "Even if — even if it works, Rigan would kill herself rather than tell you anything."

"The Morrigan will not kill herself. She will be too weak immediately after her summoning to do anything. And later she will be in irons where none of her magic will work. Whatever she knows of the Circle's plans — and she will know everything; that is the Circle's way — she will tell us."

"My pattern won't summon her." Desperately. "I'm a male, and she is not. I have none of her magic. I'm not enough like her."

"Do not hope for it, boy. If we do not succeed the first time, the Sdhe will lose his position, and then *I* will be Line-End, and forced for Line prestige to try again. We will suck you dry, boy. When we are finished there won't be anything of you left, but we will have the Morrigan."

Rigan, I'm sorry, oh, Rigan, Rigan. Dryly, humiliatingly, Arddu began to sob.

"Take him to the windsled," Menw told a waiting Red Cloak.

Iron-shod boots clattered on the copper floor. The boy was dragged out. Menw was left pacing in front of the greasy carcase he no longer wanted to eat. On the one side there was First Magic, cold and deadly, united in some secret stratagem to destroy the Line once and for all. On the other was the Sdhe, like a great scarlet spider weaving the web that would capture the Morrigan and so reveal the Circle's schemes. If the Sdhe's plan worked, the Circle could be thwarted, and the Sdhe would be Line-End for life. If it didn't, there might not be a Line left for anyone to lead.

"Either way, I lose," Menw said aloud.

As if the words were a lighted taper, he was suddenly in a rage. His magic blazed red-hot, engulfing a servient in the doorway, making her scream and tear at her forehead till the blood gouted out. That reduced his fury, but he was still simmering. He pushed the woman to one side and strode out the door.

Four interminable days by windsled to get here; at least four more to return to Uffern. Gods burn it, why couldn't he have been on his own on a missioning somewhere, instead of stuck on Nwm between First Magic and the Sdhe?

But even as he walked down the iron gangplank into the waiting windsled, even as the ship cast off, its sails turning red in the light of the sinking sun, Menw Power-Seeker was thinking again, and scheming.

FOUR

This buttress, and that one there,
More congenial around them would have been
The joy of a host,
and the tread of a minstrel.
                    — Red Book of Hergest XII

M ORGAN Lefevre turned away from the window. It had
been a daydream after all. The firepot burning, the
bearded man whose name she had known, the ancient monastery, all of it had been only a dream. She freed her wrist,
concentrating on the marks the iron buckle had left, not letting
herself look out the window again. But turning her back on
it was not enough. Even out of sight, the window dominated
the room.

In the curling twilight Morgan changed to jeans, emptied
the pockets of her shorts, carefully threw away a dirty tissue
and a broken pencil. Dusk permeated the room, absorbing
all boundaries. Hurriedly she transferred some things to her
jeans' pocket. She hesitated for a moment over the little jade
horseshoe. It felt very cold. For the first time ever she almost
didn't want to keep it with her. Defiantly she shoved it into
her pocket, and all the while the window felt like an alien
eye staring holes in her back.

She couldn't help it. She simply couldn't stop herself from
turning. Hands clenched, her back pressed hard against the
farthest wall of the room, she looked over at the window.

The glass showed a stranger wearing a long skirt and shawl.
Her eyes were huge, silver as the moon. She was beautiful
in a genderless kind of way, high cheekbones alight over the
hollows beneath, intelligent forehead brushed with brown

hair, generous mouth with finely drawn, unsmiling lips. She had a proud look, almost arrogant, but loneliness clung to her like a cloak.

Except for her brown hair, she looked exactly like Morgan.

It isn't me, Morgan thought. It can't be me.

The girl was standing on stone, a very high place with a staggering drop to the sea. Across a narrow strait was an island whose own high, flat summit was barely visible through mist. But a red flicker pierced the paleness, a firepot burning. A patch of scarlet flapped in a sudden gust of wind. The mist shredded, then blew away completely, revealing a crippled half-moon in the evening sky. From her stony eyrie the girl in the glass reached out a hand to it. It was a strange, yearning gesture, long white fingers arched toward the moon. Without understanding why, Morgan lifted her own hand, too.

Suddenly her reflection was superimposed on the other girl, one ghostly image in jeans and one in a long skirt; one with light hair and one with brown. Then the window blurred. All at once it was a whirling kaleidoscope, spinning out pale-eyed ghosts like the spokes of a wheel. Morgan twisted away from that line of faces so much like her own. But she couldn't escape seeing what was in their cupped hands. Each girl held an identical deep-blue wine cup with pearls around the rim. It was the most beautiful thing Morgan had ever seen. Her empty hands reached for it hungrily, even as she shrank away.

"What is it?" she shrilled. "What's happening to me?"

Her cry shattered the glassy images. Morgan looked down at her shaking hands. She snapped on the bedside lamp. Twilight retreated to the edges of the room, and there were no more images in the glass. A tear spilled onto her cheek. Grabbing up a jacket, she jerked open the door and ran out.

She didn't want to see anybody, so she sat on the stairs. The inn sounds came to her, the clink of cutlery, somebody's laughter, a radio playing Beethoven. The staircase was made of oak, highly polished, its wax smell obscuring the scent of the closed apple-wood door on the landing behind. The yellow brightness of the overhead light gave everything a clear and obvious boundary.

Slowly Morgan's breathing returned to normal. She checked her watch. She had plenty of time for a walk before dinner. The fresh air would do her good. Cooped up in a van all day, hardly any sleep last night, looking forward to Tintagel as if King Arthur were still alive in it and waiting for her — was it any wonder she was going a little weird?

On the second-floor landing she passed Mr. Pengelly, the innkeeper. He was a large man with a maze of wrinkles around his eyes. His voice had a hint of a Cornish accent. He was smoking a pipe. "Evening, Miss Lefay," he nodded, mispronouncing her name as everyone seemed to, here. "And what do you think of our attic room?"

"It's — fine."

"Aye. A grand view, it has. Did you see King Arthur's castle?"

She nodded. "Can you tell me how to get to the village, please? I thought I'd watch the sunset."

"You won't see much from there. Village is too far back from the headland. But if it's sunsets you're after, best ones on the whole coast are right here in our own sea garden. You can see bits of the castle from it, too." He puffed a couple of times on his pipe. Morgan remained silent. "Suit yourself, of course," he added a bit more coolly.

"The sea garden sounds nice," Morgan managed hurriedly. "How do I —?"

"Turn left at the bottom of these stairs, then go down the hall to the outside door. Bench on the hill's the best place for views."

He watched her descending the stairs. Obediently Morgan turned left, but she was in no mood for more views of the castle, and when she came to the door of the lounge, she stopped. It was a small room, full of laughter and cigarette smoke. The crew had taken all the rooms of the inn, and was obviously enjoying having a place it could call home. No one noticed Morgan hesitating in the doorway. After a moment, she continued down the long corridor. The noise faded behind her. By the time she reached the outside door, she could hear nothing. She pushed the door open and stepped out.

A zig-zag path led through a rose arbor to an overlook where a single cast-iron bench was just visible. *Hiss, gurgle, hiss,* came the sound of the sea, followed by the swooshing splash of spray. The seaweed smell overpowered even the roses. Above her head the clouds were racing. Before she let herself think, she was on the path and climbing toward the bench.

The air grew colder as she climbed, and Morgan shivered in her light jacket. She almost went back, but then she reminded herself that she had wanted to see the sunset. The last few steps were steep, and she used the iron bench to steady herself. At the top, still with one hand on the bench, she allowed herself to look.

Tintagel Castle lay before her. Morgan had read about it, had known what to expect even before she had seen it from the window of her attic room. She knew that it wasn't really a castle anymore. The knights who had gathered in its Great Hall, eating the white stag and drinking the Test of Innocence, had all been dead for more than five hundred years. Now the roof of that hall was gone, and the great stone piles of its walls had become mere bits of stone sticking up like chimneys whose houses had rotted away. Everything else from the Age of Chivalry had disappeared. And nothing at all remained of the time, centuries before that, when monks had grown their herbs on Tintagel's high plateau, and the real King Arthur had been born.

The bit of headland the castle had stood on was often called Tintagel Island, but actually a very slender neck of land, scarcely higher than sea level, joined it to the mainland. A wooden bridge had been built above the land-link, high enough to avoid the surf that regularly inundated the land below. But from here Morgan could see only the bleak cliffs of Tintagel Island rising across the cove from her, and here and there, sticking up, a column of ancient stone pierced with arrow slits.

It was very still. Behind a cloud, the sun was setting. It had been more than an hour since the landrover had collected its last weary load of passengers at the foot of the bridge and gunned its way inland back up to the village. Tintagel Island was empty, bodiless as a ghost. Morgan couldn't see her father anymore. Although the inn was just behind her, she felt very alone.

Not even a bird, she thought.

It was the still time, the time when color died. The gray ruins beckoned, gray rock and gray ocean, gray turf and gray sky. Morgan shivered. Her hand gripping the iron bench felt cold. Without thinking, she shoved both hands into her pockets.

Immediately the castle across the cove dimmed, its stones merging with the cliff, gray sheep seeming to graze where ruined walls had been. The present was fading, she was someone else . . .

She panicked, and grabbed for the iron bench again. It was too late. Suspended in time, she could see herself, her jacketed arm treacherously seeking iron, and, where the bench ought to have been, a brown-haired girl, dressed differently from Morgan and paler and straighter than she, but with features that might have been Morgan's own.

Not again, Morgan thought. Oh, please, not again.

There was a woman with the other girl. Her face had a sly kind of prettiness, and there was a curve to her robes that made Morgan wonder if she was pregnant. Her eyes said she didn't like the girl. The girl didn't like her, either. She stared at the woman, and Morgan stared with her. She'll ruin everything, Morgan thought, or the girl did, or both. She'll give up the baby and I'll never even know him.

Hatred filled her. In the gray sky a curlew screamed, wild and high. Morgan's eyes blurred. She blinked, then looked down at herself, at her twentieth-century jeans and pink jacket, at her tanned fingers spread wide on the iron bench she had finally grasped again. She looked across the cove at Tintagel. The castle ruins had returned, and there were no sheep.

Fear shivered within her. Three times now she had been taken over by someone too much like herself. She hated it, but she wanted to know more. She wanted, most of all, to know why. White-knuckled, gripping the iron bench, she stared at Tintagel. The answer to everything was over there, she knew it. All she had to do was go.

Suddenly she saw her father on the island again. He was almost exactly across from her, striding toward what seemed to be an ancient iron gate in the cliff that overlooked the cove. He waved to her. Morgan shoved her free hand into the pocket of her jeans, and her fingers closed around her lucky horseshoe. She threw back her head. Why shouldn't she go? How could it be worse over there than here?

She dropped her eyes to the ground, then let go of the bench. Hunching her shoulders forward, not allowing herself even a sidelong glance at the ruins, she began making her way down the cliff. At the bottom she found a path that skirted the cove. She followed it southward, the sky deepening, the half-moon over her shoulder already making shadows. She didn't let herself think about how late it was getting. In a few minutes she got to the foot of the bridge. Then she began to climb again.

Up she toiled, and up; it seemed to go on forever. The crumbly slope was bolstered by stairs and a handrail, and she welcomed them, because such things meant that other people besides herself came here. She tried to imagine all those real people visiting the Tintagel of the guidebooks, thousands and thousands of tourists every year. But this did not seem to be a place for tourists.

The path narrowed, the Atlantic hissing on either side. Morgan didn't let herself look down. The Pont de l'Epée, she thought, the magic bridge Sir Lancelot had taken to the Land Without Return. Narrow as the blade of a sword and spanning a boiling torrent, guarded at the other end by two horrible lions . . .

Too many books, she told herself, her breath coming in little gasps, too many late nights, too much imagination. Step after step, up and up. She never thought of turning back; she couldn't have done it, even if she had. Tintagel Island summoned her, or something did, and she could not disobey.

At last she was there. An archway led into the ruined inner ward of the castle. Briefly she saw a number of low stone walls delineating what had once been rooms. And then a mist rolled in, but it was not a mist. It crumpled the world, pleating foreground and background like a piece of paper, so that one became the other, or half of each, dimensions folding in on themselves, blending.

Morgan stood like stone, watching shapes merge, edges disappear, gray into gray, flattening. "Fog," she said, her voice loud and defensive. In its thickness she suddenly saw the ghostly image of a boy whose face was too much like her own.

"Who are you?" Morgan cried to the ghost, to all the ghosts.

But her cry was muffled in mist, and there was no iron to grasp, only the stake the boy was chained to, and that was in another world in a deep chasm beside a terrible flame, and the boy's mouth was open, and he was soundlessly screaming.

Morgan turned to flee, but the mist was behind her, too. She held out her hands imploringly, and suddenly there seemed to be a cup in them, a deep midnight-blue like the endless sea with a ring of pearls at the top; and it had all the answers, all, if only she knew the questions and could say them in time.

But she could not. She could do nothing. The mist came and took the cup, then reached for her. She couldn't stop it. Her hands went first, then her forearms. She watched it happen, mouth open in a silent scream. Like that boy, oh, God, like that boy, and burning . . .

"Dad!" she shrieked, and it came out finally, all she had time for.

And then she disappeared.

"Morgan! Where are you, you foolish girl? Morrigan!"

The Morrigan raised her gaze from the two semicircular pieces of jade in her palm. Her eyes were the color of lead. Ygerne's call had disrupted her concentration, and the mending spell was ruined. Mother rot the woman, another magic wasted!

Not that it had had much chance of success. The Morrigan had feared so from the start, slipping away from the campsite last night to this poor spell-circle of eglantine and furze, untouched by moonlight and too far from the sound of running water. She'd had to try, though. It had been her last chance to mend the circlet and use it before Ygerne fulfilled her threat and gave up her unborn babe to the Line.

"Did you hear me, Morgan?" Ygerne's voice shrilled. "I'm leaving without you. I won't wait another minute!"

But Ygerne would wait; she had no choice. To pay the M'rlendd for magically removing her second and as yet unborn child, she would be giving him the Morrigan as maidservant. For Ygerne, the only thing that mattered was to prevent her long-absent husband from discovering he had been cuckolded. In such a circumstance she would have done far worse than offer up her firstborn child as a magician's slave.

Ygerne had always disliked the Morrigan. Even at the moment of her birth, the look of the baby's pale, old eyes had disgusted her mother. When, later, the nurse had spoken of the two pieces of jade the child had spat out and which afterward had apparently disappeared, Ygerne's dislike of the baby had increased to fear. She didn't acknowledge her fear even to herself, but the Morrigan knew. The Morrigan had known it from the beginning.

Ygerne had named her Morrigan. That much the Circle had known. But then she had decided Morrigan was too grand a name, suiting the stiff, proud girl a little too well. And so she had become Morgan, as diminished in name as she was not in spirit. It was a foolish battle that Ygerne and the Morrigan continued to fight, this fifteen-year-old child who was not a child, and this mother who was no mother. The Morrigan knew she wasted herself on it.

She had too little else to do, that was the trouble. All these years on Earth she had had no real labor except to learn the Earth substitutes for Nwmish things, to strive with the broken circlet, and to darken her hair against the time when she would first encounter the M'rlendd. She could do nothing about the color of her eyes, but among other gray-eyed people of Earth her own didn't seem too odd. With her hair dyed brown and her parentage on this world well known, not even the M'rlendd would guess she was a First Magic Sister from Nwm.

Still on her knees, the Morrigan now put the broken jade pieces back into the girdle of her skirt. Another failure, she thought. Fifteen years of failing, of living with a broken magic and being unable to mend it; fifteen years of this dreary world with its struggling moon and its blending seasons. She got to her feet, methodically grinding the spell-herbs beneath her sandals. Without the jade circlet her own magic was not strong enough to stop Ygerne from handing her unborn child over to the M'rlendd. And though the broken pieces of jade would each bear some magic of their own, they would not be enough to compete against a Linesman.

All this time waiting and waiting for Ygerne to conceive the boy whose future would be so important to Earth, only to have the M'rlendd calmly step in and take the babe for himself before it was even born! The boy would survive, of course. He would grow up on the M'rlendd's island in the solitary *care of a Linesman, and when he came into his own he would bring his world into Alignment, not Encircling. And she, who had been trained her whole life and allowed herself to be missioned into an Earth-woman's womb in order to be that boy's sister and teacher, was left with no chance of influencing him.*

Unless she let herself be abandoned with the boy. Unless she stayed on the M'rlendd's island and let herself seem to serve a Linesman.

Slowly the Morrigan left her makeshift spell-circle, then made her way out to the campsite. Ygerne's mute servant was already holding the donkey's head, and Ygerne herself was mounted. She was buxom and fair and wore her clothes well, so that few people had guessed her condition.

"So there you are, Morgan!" she called sharply. "And out all night, by the state of your skirts. Do you not care what you look like?"

The Morrigan allowed herself one insolent look at Ygerne's own skirts. Then she shrugged. "I am here now. Ride if you will. I'll follow."

It was almost noon before they were in sight of the sea. Northward along the coast the Morrigan could make out a head-shaped island very near the mainland. A surprising nervousness possessed her. Who would have thought the M'rlendd would pick an island for his headquarters? On Nwm such places were invariably First Magic. What confidence this Linesman must have!

It was early, but still she called up her strongest mental shield. She let herself become an ordinary Earth-girl, daughter of Ygerne. She suppressed her magic so that there would be nothing to arouse the M'rlendd's suspicions. It was a frightening feeling, being so far removed from her own powers. She let herself be frightened, knowing it was what the M'rlendd would expect from a young Earth-girl approaching him for the first time.

The afternoon wore away, and the island drew near. Now that they were close enough, she could see that there was actually a land link between the cliffs of the mainland and the so-called island. Seeing the neck of land joining the two,

47

the Morrigan's spirits rose a little. The M'rlendd was not quite so daring after all. Still, there was something about that narrow ridge of land that disturbed her. The M'rlendd's stronghold was neither true island nor true mainland. When a thing was neither First Magic nor Second, whose was the advantage?

They stopped on the mainland, a high stony place overlooking the narrow land bridge below. The Morrigan eyed Ygerne. She was smiling, pleased that soon she would be free of the child she bore. Did she have no sense of the vileness of what she was doing? How could anyone give up a baby?

Across the bay, mist was rolling in, but visible in it was a small flash of moving scarlet that must be the M'rlendd. He was waiting for them.

Carefully they made their way down to the surf-tossed neck of land that led to the M'rlendd's stronghold. The Morrigan trailed the others. Without warning, fear attacked her. Something was wrong. Her steps grew slower. She stopped. A magic was reaching for her. It was shaped in her pattern, and it did not come from the island. It was Second Magic.

A Second Magic summoning! Somehow the Line was using her own pattern to summon her back to Nwm!

Her shield almost failed. Again the reaching came, and again she resisted. Shock and horror kept her motionless on the slippery land bridge. Her shield was in tatters. She knew she could not withstand another attempt. Doomstruck, she waited for it, but the attempt never came. The summoning moved on, and her pattern went with it, seeking her through all time.

How had the Line found her pattern?

Or had they perhaps found a pattern that was so much like hers, it might have been her own?

Arddu, she thought. Oh, my brother.

Ahead of her, Ygerne called her name. With a wrench the Morrigan renewed her shield. She was soaked with sweat, but she made herself go on. For her fifteen years on Earth it had been as if she had no brother, as if Arddu was dead. Now he was dead, or as good as. The Line had used him to try to get her, and it would not enjoy its failure.

It did not occur to her to wonder why the men of the Line hadn't succeeded in drawing her back to Nwm. They had not; that was all that mattered. She followed Ygerne up the path, and her mind was set on the task ahead, on the Linesman who must be fooled, on the male who would learn from her the meaning of a Sister's service. But deeper still, deeper than anything, was the ghost of her brother, Arddu. The only thing she could do for Arddu was to avenge him. She must hurt the Line as much as possible.

I will make them pay, she vowed. The Line will not win Earth, Arddu. Whatever happens, whatever I must do, the Line will not win Earth.

FIVE

Death above our head,
Wide is its covering.
— Book of Taliessin IX
   (Juvenile Ornaments of
   Taliessin)

I N the desert of eastern Nwm, where the moon was a servient's enemy and the sun his dread, where even the deepest wells had to be kept covered, where only the windsleds
and the nomads came and went, somehow two cities thrived.
They faced each other across a deep canyon. Uffern was on
the eastern side, a many-towered city, hotly colored. On the
west, directly linked to Uffern by the iron bridge only the
Line ever used, was the hunkering bulk of Bryn Tyddwl.

The canyon that separated the cities went for leagues to
the north and south, but its deepest part lay between them.
Here the smooth canyon walls descended vertically to the
blue slate flatness of what might once have been a river valley.
About a quarter league across that valley, halfway between
the canyon walls, the level ground was slashed by a deep,
narrow gorge. It was this chasm, cracked and broken by the
torrid heat of the fires burning in its depths, that fed the
Line's Magic. The iron bridge that hung above it was the only
place in Nwm where Linesmen worked easily as a unit. When
that happened, the smoke from the chasm could be seen as
far away as Ystavingon, and the servients of all the east averted
their eyes and called it a bad day.

Today had been a bad day. For no one had it been worse
than for Arddu A'Casta.

He lay motionless in his chains beneath the bridge, awake but with no strength left for fighting. Second Magic was everywhere in him, peering into his deepest parts, making a template out of him. Staying conscious through it was almost more than he could bear. But somehow he had managed it. Fuzzily he knew it gave him something the Linesmen could not take. He hoped it would enrage them. He wanted them to order his death.

But of course they did not. Even the Line could not dissect the pattern from a corpse.

At noon, when the terrible sun was at its highest and the fires roared like demons in the chasm, they gave him water. He tried not to drink it, but the will that kept his mind conscious seemed to have no control over his body. He even sought the shameful shade of the bridge, doggedly crawling to the limits of his chain while the Linesmen watched with curiosity. As the day passed, the sweat dried off his body almost before it had a chance to form, and his silver eyes turned a strange, tarnished pewter. More than one Linesman wondered if he would die before his sister could be summoned.

"We have garnered enough of him," the Sdhe said at last.

He was at the front of the Line, old, though his rich brown skin was scarcely lined and his shoulders were still powerful under the scarlet cloak. His tunic was striated with the gleaming iron threads that held it together. Fire-opals studded his sash, and his thick neck-torc of gold glittered. He was all that was Uffern, all that was Second Magic. He looked unconquerable.

Nonetheless, Menw Power-Seeker objected. "There is some incompleteness."

"It is enough," the Sdhe insisted. "On Earth only the Morrigan can have a pattern so much like this boy's. Only she can possibly respond to it."

The summoning began.

They knew neither the Morrigan's specific location on Earth nor exactly how many Earth-years had passed in the days since her missioning from Nwm. It was of no significance. They sent the boy's essence through all the lands and ages of Earth. Suddenly they encountered resistance. They stiffened

51

and tried again. Twice the energy pattern glanced aside like a spear off a shield. Then, almost too easily, contact was made.

In unison the Line contracted, a single powerful jerk like a rope tugging. Below them in the canyon the A'Casta's back arched in agony. A form took shape in the smoke from the chasm, a young, pale female in strange garments of pink and blue. Her face was almost identical to the boy's. The Line moved her to the iron chains waiting for her near him.

Men moved slightly away from one another. There were a few gloating murmurs. A Sister surrounded by iron, a Sister whose magic was now useless to her. A Sister who could kill neither herself nor anything else. A Sister whose mind, and everything in it, would soon be theirs.

On the bridge, the Sdhe's crossed arms stroked one another. He was eyeing the female narrowly. Now and then his eyes flicked toward her pink jacket.

Arddu stirred. For the first time in hours his mind was free of the Line. He knew why. Slowly he dragged his aching body up, turning his head, trying to see through the fog that clung to his eyes. *Rigan? Rigan, are you here?*

There was another stake, farther away from the bridge than his own. Someone was chained there, a supine body, motionless. Rigan? He couldn't tell. Only her clothing was clear to him, and everything about it was wrong. Surely a Sister of the First Magic would never choose such colors! Pink was too close to red, and blue . . .

He turned his gaze to the men on the bridge, all dark-haired and blue-eyed, all flickering in their firelit scarlet and gold. They were still in Line, but even Arddu could sense their separateness as they eyed one another. It was like wolves, he thought, checking for dominance after a group kill. For the first time he understood why Linesmen who took weapons into their hands invariably lost their magic. There would have been no Line left if Linesmen had been allowed to kill.

Again he strained toward that motionless form that might be Rigan. He said nothing aloud, but his mind shouted questions at her, begging her to answer him. There was no response at all. If she was Rigan, something had changed her, making her voiceless and uncomprehending.

The sinking sun made a single line out of the Linesmen's shadows. The fire in the chasm had almost gone out. But in the growing gloom Menw Power-Seeker had been watching the girl carefully. "The Morrigan's mind is silent," he said, after a long time. It was an accusation. "Even unconscious, she should react somehow."

Farther down the Line, another man said doubtfully, "Do you think her mind is gone?" In the chasm an ember hissed, and a lick of flame went up, revealing the Sdhe's expressionless face.

"If that is so," Menw pointed out, "we will never learn what the Circle is scheming. All of this will have been for nothing."

The Sdhe's cloak caught the light with a reptilian shimmer. A tiny jerk of movement, Arddu thought; almost invisible, if his cloak had not given him away.

"The Morrigan has been summoned by a magic not her own," the Sdhe said blandly. "All she needs is time to recover."

"To recover her own mind, perhaps," Menw insinuated softly. "But the Morrigan's?"

The Sdhe's eyes slitted. "Perhaps the A'Casta should identify his sister for us, as Power-Seeker seems to think that is necessary."

Arddu felt himself lifted to his feet, though no hands touched him. Energy poured into his being. Though he still had his arms chained, he was somehow closer to the girl and could now see her clearly.

She had Rigan's face and Rigan's long sweep of hair, though perhaps a little less fair than before. Her eyes were closed. He thought the lashes might be too dark, but he had rarely seen Rigan asleep, so how could he be sure? Her face was browner than he remembered. But he had heard that people were always a little changed after a missioning. He lifted a heavy arm to his eyes and rubbed them, chains jangling.

"Well?" It was a Linesman's voice.

She had always been slender, but now she seemed almost too thin. And to have allowed herself to become unconscious! Where was her power? This was not the Rigan he knew.

He looked up at the Sdhe. A message, hot and deadly, was in the Line-End's eyes.

Arddu's tongue felt too big for his mouth. *If we do not succeed the first time . . .* Another day like this one, another and another. *We will suck you dry.* If that wasn't Rigan lying over there . . . *In the end there will not be anything of you left.* And in the end, too, it would be Rigan lying there.

Maybe it was Rigan, anyway. He wasn't sure. He wasn't sure of anything.

Menw was looking at him. "The A'Casta is surprised by her," he said, when Arddu was silent. His eyes were like the blue heart of a flame. "Is that not true, boy? You do not think she is — herself."

Arddu knew the fiery probe of Second Magic. He knew, too, that someone else's Second Magic was helping him resist it. "How could she be herself?" he said belligerently. "No one touched by the Line can remain undefiled."

The words were not his own. Someone else had made him say them. Again his gaze brushed the Sdhe's, the one man who would lose as much as Arddu if this girl should not prove to be the Morrigan.

"Try another answer, boy," a Linesman said.

Arddu managed a sulky tone. "She is sick, an Earth illness. She would not have come when you summoned, otherwise." Again, someone else's words. Arddu looked at the Sdhe, his stomach churning with fear.

"I would rather believe she is not of the Circle at all than believe a Sister could be sick," Menw said.

The Sdhe raised his brows. "Are you truly accusing me of error, Line-Second? This female's brother has identified her. He has given a valid reason both for her mental silence and the ease we felt in summoning her. Do you wish to present proof that he lies, and that I have erred by leading in the summoning of the wrong female?"

For a moment no one seemed to breathe. Then Menw said reluctantly, "I spoke hastily. It is possible that even a Sister might not be able to self-cure a disease of the outworlds." He gave an ironic bow. "And, of course, it is the Sdhe's fame that he makes no errors."

Smiling, the Sdhe turned his gaze toward Arddu. "Has dwelling with the Circle taught you any healing that might help the Morrigan over this Earth sickness?"

"I can't help her from here," Arddu got out. "You'd have to let me be near enough to touch her." He was like a puppet, he thought, the words tugged out of him by someone else's strings.

"So be it," the Sdhe said calmly. "The two prisoners will be chained together. At the next sun we will all reconvene here to question the Morrigan. Until then, I leave their safety in the capable hands of Menw Power-Seeker." He grinned suddenly, a sharp-toothed look that made Arddu shudder.

In the west the sun was sinking rapidly. Bryn Tyddwl haunted the canyon's rim, its watchfires blinking red eyes out of the murk. To the east Uffern was lit up in defiance of the night. The Sdhe began to walk toward it along the swaying, groaning bridge. After a moment the rest of the Line followed, gold cloak after red, red after gold, opulent and oppressive. Menw went with them, though first directing a quick jerk of the head to the girl and Arddu. With a dizzying dislocation Arddu found himself tied to the same iron stake that tethered the girl. The flood of energy that had kept him on his feet drained away. He slumped to his knees.

"Rigan?" he whispered. It was all he could manage. There was no answer, only the soft sigh of her breathing.

Above their heads the last man in Line disappeared into lamplit Uffern. They were alone in the chasm, as alone as the iron and the fire would allow. And Arddu didn't trust it, not for a minute.

★

It was a hot, dry place, acrid with old smoke. Morgan Lefevre raised her head, blinking out into a night dim with the flicker of smoldering fires. She had been going to King Arthur's island. Where was she now? Her throat ached for water. Licking her lips, she let her head fall back, and overhead she saw something suspended, a skeletal structure of iron. A bridge? Her arms were twisted behind her, and they hurt, a pin cushion of aches and numbness. She tried to move them and heard the jangle of chain.

Behind her back someone moaned.

Panicked, Morgan jerked away. But there were chains around her wrists and a stake behind her and she couldn't get away. The faceless presence moaned again.

"Who are you?" she got out, a cracked whisper only. "Tell me!"

Arddu dragged himself out of the only sleep he'd had in two days. Groggily he sat up. It was the middle of the night. The stake felt hard and hostile between his shoulder blades. Back to back with him, the stake in between, the girl was awake at last. "Who are you?" she was whispering. Panic was in her voice, in her mind. He felt it, and knew. She was not Rigan.

Joy rose in him, but he clamped it down. Rigan was somewhere else, free and alive and out of reach of the Line. He had to keep her that way. But there were only a few hours left before the Linesmen would try to question this girl. How could he keep them from finding her out? Even now they might be watching.

"Quiet," he hissed, but she didn't seem to hear. Her voice was getting more frantic. Arddu struggled in his chains, turning himself around, reaching a manacled hand to cover the girl's mouth. She twisted away. In the chasm a small volcano erupted, a trail of sparks lighting the sky. Now they could see each other, alike as two twins.

Morgan went still. Someone else with her face. She was asleep. She was dreaming. But her wrists burned where the iron had cut, and — God! — there was that strange silver moon whirling like a top in a sky full of the wrong stars, and her eyes were open, and she knew, she *knew* she was not asleep.

"I — I — where am — Mom? *Mom?*"

Arddu had heard every one of her thoughts as clearly as if she had been Rigan. There was no time to try to understand it. This girl would be screaming in a moment. He had to do something. Nervously he reached out for her with his mind.

You're in Nwm — you've been brought here in mistake for my sister. But she looked at him dumbly, blind with fear. He could hear her mind, but she couldn't hear his. Disappointed, yet relieved, he grabbed her roughly.

"Listen to me!" he whispered. "This isn't your world. It's Nwm. The Line summoned you from Earth in mistake for my sister. You've got to pretend you *are* her, or they'll kill us both trying for her again." Loudly, for unseen listeners, he added, "Are you feeling better, Rigan?"

"Rigan?" she asked, loud and uncooperative.

"Don't you remember your own name? You're the Morrigan, a Sister of the First Magic. You're my sister. Was the summoning that bad, that you don't remember?" Arddu was shaking. So now he had given her memory loss to live up to!

She rubbed her forehead, the chains clanking. In her mind Arddu saw an island raw and gray under a pale crescent moon, a headland bare of trees. Was that what Earth was like? How Rigan must hate it! And he saw in the girl's mind a dark-haired man with eyes as blue as the sea, and a woman pacing fearfully in front of him. *Mom, oh, Mom,* the girl's thoughts wept, and for the first time since she had come, Arddu pitied her.

"Pretend to be sick," he whispered. "You've got to. Please."

She stared at him for a long moment, then coughed violently. In the echo she whispered, "How come you look so much like me?"

He leaned forward, pretending to check for fever. "Rigan's my twin," he whispered back. "She looks like me — like you, too. Your pattern must be almost the same as ours."

"Pattern? You mean, genes?"

Over their heads the bridge swayed suddenly. Loudly and desperately, Arddu said, "Don't try to remember it all now, Rigan. It'll come back to you if you —"

"I don't think," said a new, dry voice from overhead, "I don't think we need maintain this fiction any longer, Arddu A'Casta. We both know this is not the Morrigan."

And with a sinking heart Arddu looked up and saw the Sdhe.

SIX

Let the face of the ground be turned up,
Let the assailants be covered,
When chiefs repair to the toil of war.
— Red Book of Hergest XI

M ENW Power-Seeker padded uneasily through Uffern. Around him the metal keeps soared into the night, loud with the twang of unilharps. Red smokes curled from firepots on the window ledges, and fiery reflections licked the shining iron paths at his feet. In the hard glitter of the night Menw hunched moodily into his cloak. He had been walking for some time, chewing over the humiliation he had suffered on the bridge. It had been stupid to challenge the Sdhe without proof; he must make no such mistake again. Yet he was sure the summoned female was not the Morrigan. And he was almost sure that the Sdhe knew it, too.

And if that were so, what serpent's egg of a scheme was the Sdhe hatching, to prevent the rest of the Line finding out?

He paused at an intersection where three paths met. One led to the bridge over the chasm. He looked at it but didn't move, not even when a window-fire billowed acrid fumes into his face. He was thinking of other kinds of smoke screens.

The summoned female chained to her supposed brother so that the boy might heal her illness. No herbs and no tools, the boy magicless, and she, supposedly First Magic, unable to heal herself.

The whole thing stank like a corpse in the desert.

So, why chain them together at all?

Suddenly Menw knew why. He pounded a fist into the wall. Alive, the girl was proof that the Sdhe had erred. But dead? Dead, the evidence would be gone. No one would ever have to know that she was not the Morrigan.

Of course the Sdhe couldn't kill the girl himself. But he didn't need to. He had a puppet chained to the girl, a boy-puppet whose powers of resistance were almost gone. Even so, the boy was no natural murderer. He would have to be forced. Mental influence, the strength of Second Magic — which meant the Sdhe would have to be there, too.

A concentrating, well-occupied Sdhe.

A Sdhe who might not be prepared for danger from the rear.

Menw Power-Seeker turned swiftly into the path that led to the bridge. After a moment, like a hunter, he began to run.

★

"We both know that this is not the Morrigan."

Up on a bridge, silhouetted against the night, the Sdhe was devoid of color, a bat-shape. Only his face was clear, his eyes reflecting the fire in the canyon so that they seemed almost to burn with their own light.

Arddu dragged himself to his knees. His heart was pounding. "So you know," he said. His voice was too shrill.

"Who is he?" the girl said, tugging on his arm. "Who is that man?"

"I am the Sdhe," he said, smiling brilliantly down at her. "You should know the name of the last Linesman you will ever see."

The girl's fingernails were digging into Arddu's arm. Her thoughts were closed to him.

"Linesmen can't kill," Arddu said, "and you haven't brought any Red Cloaks to do it for you."

"I need no Red Cloaks, A'Casta," said the Sdhe. "I have you."

The girl let out a strangled cry and moved away from Arddu as far as their shared chain allowed.

"Me?" Arddu choked. "The Line will never believe I would kill —"

"If this girl really were a Sister of the First Magic, she would beg you for death, rather than reveal anything to us. And you, as her true brother, would grant her wish, out of love for her."

"I wouldn't! I —"

Sudden as a thunderclap the fire roared up. In its glare the Sdhe's arms stabbed out at Arddu from under his cloak. Arddu felt heat slash through his skull. His mouth slackened, and his eyes went dull. He turned in his chains and looked at the girl.

She stared back at him. "It's not fair," she cried. "I didn't ask to be brought here. I don't even know your sister. It's not fair!"

"I won't do it," Arddu declared. But his lips didn't move. Disbelievingly, he looked at his hands. There was a length of chain looped up in them. And then, jerkily, that loop began to move toward the girl's neck.

★

"It's a way out, boy." The Sdhe's voice, winding into his mind. "If they believe she was Rigan, the real Rigan will be dead to them. Your sister will be safe. If it costs this girl's death, remember, she would die anyway. This way, her death will have meaning."

Truth. Hard to resist.

Scratches on his face, fingernails like claws. Feet kicking at him, bruising. But she was not as strong as he was. She would not outlast him. And she was chained to him. She couldn't escape.

He felt moisture on the back of one hand. She was crying, he thought in surprise. His hands slackened on the iron chain.

"She is a stranger to you, boy. You owe her nothing. And with her death you will save your sister."

Save Rigan? He'd never done that. It was always she who'd had to save him.

Rigan would not have wept as this girl did. Yet her neck was so like Rigan's, long and slender and white.

"Your sister would have done it for you, boy."

"I am not my sister!" Arddu wailed despairingly, even as once again his hands tightened on the iron.

★

Menw reached the eastern edge of the bridge just as the chasm fire leaped up. In the distant glare he could make out someone crouched on the central walkway, leaning out into the canyon with one steadying arm on a girder. The metallic stink of the other's Second Magic wafted Menw's way, even from so far away. Gods, the Sdhe was powerful!

Silent as a hunting cat, Menw stole down the bridge. The Sdhe was arrowing his magic straight downward, pouring it into the boy in the canyon. Closer. Closer. The Sdhe's cloak filled Menw's eyes like blood, but still he kept going. The Sdhe did not take his eyes off the boy in the canyon below.

Here, Menw thought. Carefully he braced himself against an iron support on the north side of the walkway. The Sdhe was still leaning out to the south. With a curse and a prayer, Menw opened his mind.

Magic poured out. The Sdhe jerked. "What —?" He tried to turn, to swing his deadly blue eyes Menw's way. But Menw's magic beat him back. The Sdhe's supporting arm slid along the girder as if it were oiled. His body, delicately balanced, overcompensated. One foot slid off the walkway, then the other.

"Power-Seeker!" he wailed, long and terrible. Then he was gone.

★

Arddu slumped back against the iron post, shaking so violently even his vision was blurred. "Are you all right?" he chattered out. "Girl? *Girl?*"

There was no answer. He wanted to reach for her, but didn't, remembering that other time, and the chain he had held. Instead he scrubbed at his eyes.

"It's all right. You didn't kill me." Her eyes were huge. There were marks on her throat.

61

"I didn't mean to hurt you," he choked out, staring at the marks. "I tried not to."

"I know. How did you — stop him?"

With one accord, they looked up. The man on the bridge looked back at them, smiling faintly. It was not the Sdhe.

"Menw Power-Seeker!" Arddu gasped.

"You may call me Line-End," Menw said. He jerked his head toward an oozing red bundle on the slate below the bridge. "The Sdhe has — had an accident." He waved his arm, a complicated pattern like a tracing of flame.

Arddu heard the clank of iron on slate. He held out his hands, gaping at the place where the manacles had been. Free, he thought. He shook his head in disbelief. Surely Menw didn't intend to let the two of them go?

"What are *you* going to do with us?" It was the girl who said it, speaking Arddu's question for him. She got to her feet.

Menw frowned consideringly at her. "You look more like a Sister now," he remarked.

Arddu said desperately, "You're not going to try another summoning?!"

"It was the Sdhe's plan to summon the Morrigan, not mine. Why should I risk my position on something that has already failed once?"

"But Line prestige — you said you'd have to keep trying!"

"The Line will discover the Sdhe's body here," Menw said. "They will be shocked; they will wonder why he came. I will suggest that he was disturbed by my apparent belief that this girl was not the Morrigan. I will suggest that he came here to test the girl, to prove that I was wrong. He would have been sure that even the Morrigan could not defeat a Line-End in this place of Line power. And so he would have loosed her chains, because no test of First Magic is possible near iron. But to his surprise he would have found that the Morrigan's magic was mightier than his own. Destroyed by her Spelled Death, his corpse fell from the bridge."

"But it didn't happen that way," the girl protested. "We'll tell them —"

"He isn't going to let us tell them," Arddu interrupted.

Menw's voice was calm. "You are the Morrigan, girl. You are free of your chains. You would never let yourself be chained again. The Line will not be able to question you now. You are useless alive, and you have killed our Line-End. And so you must be killed in return: a servient death, quick and distant."

"But I'm not the Morrigan!" the girl wailed suddenly.

"You are now," Menw said. "Enjoy it while it lasts." And with only a flicker of flame to mark his passing, he was gone.

★

"We've got to do something! Boy. Hey! Get up!"

"My name is Arddu," he said, not looking at her. He was sitting with his back to the stake, hugging his knees.

"That man called you something else. The A'Cast—?"

"Arddu," he repeated coldly.

"Arddu." She was on her feet, stamping the numbness out, rubbing her arms. No part of her body was still. "What are we going to do?" she demanded. "They're coming back at dawn. And you're just sitting around like you —"

"Listen, whatever your name is, you don't know anything about it."

"Morgan. My name's Morgan."

"Morgan, Morrigan," he muttered. "Gods, even your names are —"

"Please! Arddu! Can't we get out of here?"

"Do you really think Menw would have unchained us if we could? We can't climb out of this canyon. And as long as we're in it, they're bound to find us. There's nowhere to hide down here. There's nothing but the slate and the chasm and the bridge."

She blinked into the darkness. "I don't know how you can be so sure. I can't see a thing."

So she was as night-blind as a servient. He couldn't help himself. "Rigan could see at night. She saw better at night than in the day."

"Well, I'm not Rigan!" she snapped. Then, "We really can't climb out of this canyon?"

"The cliffs are like glass."

63

"Steep, or only slippery?"

"Like this." He held his arms up, nearly vertical. "And not a handhold anywhere."

"There must be somewhere —"

"Listen — Morgan," Arddu said, stumbling over her name. "I've heard all about this canyon. It goes for leagues, and only in the far north is there anywhere we could climb out. It would take us days to walk there, and we haven't got days. And there's no water anywhere. Even without Menw sending his Red Cloaks along the rim looking for us, we'd die of thirst before we could get out."

She jerked her hair. "Well, I'm not going to just wait for them to kill me. I'd rather jump off that bridge!"

"You can't get up there," Arddu pointed out sourly.

They looked at it, its iron glitter hanging so far out of reach. "Where does it go to?" Morgan asked.

"What difference does it make? I've told you and told you, we can't get out of here."

"I only asked where the bridge went."

He was too tired to argue. "East to Uffern, west to Bryn Tyddwl. The Line owns them both, so even if we could climb up —"

"What's beyond Uffern and — that other place?"

Her stubbornness was making it harder and harder for Arddu to sit still. Rigidly, enunciating every word, he said, "East of Uffern is desert. No roads, nobody ever goes there. The Line owns it all. West of Bryn Tyddwl is Eifionydd. It's a huge plain, mostly desert. There are a few roads, but the Line owns them all. The Line owns everythng in eastern Nwm. There isn't the slightest chance that we'll ever get away. You had better accept it."

Slowly she sat down. Her shoulders slumped. She hugged her knees to her chest, not looking at him. Her face was in shadow. He could hear nothing in her mind. Irrationally, her despair disturbed him more than her questions.

He cleared his throat. "Western Nwm," he said, "now, that's different." She didn't look up. "It's owned by the Circle — that's First Magic. Female, like Rigan." Still no reaction.

He tried again. "The Line is Second Magic. Second Magic and First Magic have always hated each other."

She lifted her face to his. "Why are you telling me this?"

He didn't know. "To pass the time?" He shrugged.

"Oh," she said dully. Then, with an effort he admired, she said, "Your sister — why did the Line want to get her from Earth?"

"To question her. They think the Circle has a plan to destroy them, and they wanted Rigan to tell them what it was."

"Wouldn't it have been easier to question somebody who was already here?"

"Circle members don't let themselves be taken alive. But in a summoning they're too disoriented to defend themselves. The Line might have tried summoning before this, but they needed a pattern. And they didn't have one, not until they got me."

Slowly Morgan asked, "Your pattern is really so much like Rigan's?"

"It must be even more like yours."

It was a disturbing thought, one she didn't like any more than he did. Arddu could see it in her face. He got to his feet, then kicked at their chain, lying loosely on the ground beside the stake. "Iron," he muttered, with a loathing not aimed entirely at the chain.

"Iron's magic, isn't it?" she said.

He looked at her in surprise. How did she know? Once again her mind opened to him. He saw an iron buckle strapped to Morgan's wrist, a wide seascape sky. He saw a man, bearded, blue-eyed, stirring a firepot. And then, suddenly, he saw a girl, brown-haired but indisputably Rigan. Shaken, Arddu blinked at Morgan. She knew Rigan! Why hadn't she told him?

She shifted uncomfortably under his eyes. "Don't look like that," she said. "I was just guessing about iron."

He could hardly tell her that he could read her mind. He wanted to know about Rigan, but he couldn't think of any way to ask. "You weren't just guessing," he accused her.

"All right, I wasn't! It'll sound crazy, but I'll tell you. I've been having dreams. Today — yesterday? — anyway, it was on Earth — I kept dreaming about a girl. She looked a lot like me. Like both of us." Slowly and miserably she added, "When I touched iron, it stopped me from dreaming, so it had to be magic. Anyway, who cares? We're going to be dead soon." She shoved up one of her sleeves. Dejectedly she looked at her wrist. "My watch has stopped."

"Your what?"

"It doesn't matter."

Her voice was thick. She wouldn't look at him. Arddu knew she was crying. Savagely he kicked at the chain. The two loose ends jangled together. He kicked it, again and again. Gods rot Menw. And the Sdhe lying there, his head smashed, his torc looking like a hook buried in bloody meat.

A hook.

A hook at the end of a chain.

Wildly, he turned his eyes up to the bridge. How far was it, gods, how far? He grabbed up one end of the chain, hefting it in his hand. It was light for its strength. For the first time he blessed Second Magic inventiveness. Hardly daring to breathe, he began to measure it out.

"What are you doing?" Morgan asked. "Arddu? What are you doing?"

It was long. Easily long enough. He gave a whoop of pure joy.

She scrambled to her feet. "Arddu? What —?"

Ruthlessly, Arddu went over to the Sdhe's body and yanked off his torc. It was solid gold. Soft, but strong, too. Its shape was a broken circle. Arddu put his foot on one of the ends and clasped the other with both hands. Then, grunting with effort, he began to pull. Bit by bit the opening between the tapered ends widened. At last it would open no farther.

"It's a hook," he told Morgan, grinning ferociously, willing it to be so. "If only the ends are narrow enough . . ."

He ran over to the end of the chain. Praying, he jammed one end of the torc at the final link of the chain. Go in, he urged it, go in! It did. He jammed the torc in farther. At last it stopped, wedged too firmly to be budged. With the back of one hand he wiped off his cheeks.

He turned to Morgan. "Can you climb a hanging chain?"

She gave a wild little laugh. "To get out of here? Just you watch me."

"I'll have to," he said. "I'll be right behind you." Then he coiled up the chain, aimed at one of the bridge's support cables, and threw.

SEVEN

It broke out with matchless fury . . .
Fire, the fiery meteor of the dawn.
— Book of Taliessin XXV

H E got it on the third attempt, hooking the Sdhe's torc around an iron girder supporting the bridge's central walkway. Caressing the dangling end of the chain, he grinned uneasily. "Circle luck," he said.

"What?" Morgan asked.

"The luck of threes. Something I'm not supposed to have."

"Why not?"

"The Circle doesn't like me." He leaned all his weight on the chain, praying it would hold. It did.

"I thought your sister was in the Circle," Morgan said.

"What's that got to do with it?" He tugged one last time on the chain. "Looks solid," he said. "You ready?"

Morgan looked up at the chain. Iron. Second Magic. She thrust her chin out. Second Magic had done enough to her, dropping her into this crazy world with its chasms and fires and hatreds that had nothing to do with her. And all because she happened to look like Arddu's sister. All to save the face of one Linesman who had already killed one man and would have her killed, too, if she didn't take hold of this chain right now. She took a deep breath, fixed her eyes on the moon, and reached for the chain.

It felt hot. Her arms jerked up, sneaker-clad feet wriggling desperately for a toehold. The chain swung back and forth, even with Arddu's weight below to steady it. Legs crossed, muscles clenching, she shinnied upward.

"Keep going," she heard from behind her when she slowed. "If you stop even for a moment you'll give up."

And she remembered how a long time ago someone else had said that to her, in gym class, when she'd been climbing a monkey net. For marks, she marveled, that was all, just for marks.

They rested when they reached the bridge. Sprawled on a webbing of thick cables beside the walkway, they lay panting and quivering, unable to believe they had really done it.

Except that we haven't, Morgan thought. We've only gotten out of that canyon. And the Line was coming back at dawn, and already the night was thinning. "Where to now?" she said raggedly, dragging herself to her knees.

"West," Arddu said. "We'll try to find somewhere to hide near Bryn Tyddwl until tomorrow night. After that, who knows?"

He scrambled to his feet on one of the girders, unhooked the Sdhe's torc and threw the chain down. He offered her a hand, but Morgan made her own way over to the walkway, crawling until the footing was secure. Then she got to her feet.

The walkway was just wide enough for two. It shone with a reddish light, its iron tiles fitting together like snake scales. Arddu was already heading west. She hurried to keep up with him. It was like walking on a cookie sheet. No matter how carefully they stepped, the bridge rattled and echoed around them. Above and below, like an asthmatic breath, a hot wind whistled.

"Why did you keep that man's torc?" she asked after a few minutes.

"We couldn't leave it attached to the chain, or they'd have guessed right away we'd used it to get up here."

"Won't they notice he isn't wearing his torc?"

"Maybe not. Even if they do, unless they see the link between a missing torc and that chain, they'll be bound to think we're still in the canyon."

"But Menw's going to say I'm the Morrigan. Why wouldn't somebody think that her magic could have got us up here?"

"First Magic couldn't get us up to an iron bridge. Menw will say we're heading for the stony parts of the canyon north of here. That's where Rigan would be able to use her magic."

For a while they walked in silence. Morgan was thinking hard. "That torc's gold," she said finally. "If there are guards at the end of this bridge, could we use it to bribe them?"

"Not unless you want to meet Menw again," he said grimly. "Only Linesmen wear torcs. Anyone we offered it to would know where we got it."

The bridge swayed and creaked, echoing with their hurrying footsteps. In the north the mad moon whirled. Would it ever set, Morgan wondered, or would it continue circling all the while the sun rose and fell? Crazy, she thought, this whole world is crazy. No rules, nothing to fall back on. A world of unscreened windows.

After what seemed like forever, a few lights pricked the gloom ahead, some distance to the right of the bridge. They were widely spaced and had the gusty look of outdoor flames. "Watchfires," Arddu whispered. "And nobody to tend them."

"Nobody?"

"Not in Bryn Tyddwl. Not until sunrise. It's a Line City, and people who belong to the Line don't go out at night unless they're forced."

"Anyway, it looks like we won't be going right into the city. Or doesn't this bridge keep going straight?"

Arddu grunted. "In Line territory everything man-made is straight."

So there were rules after all, Morgan thought. Second Magic liked iron and straight lines and hated the night. She looked over her shoulder at distant Uffern, all its brilliant lights now blended to one small, glittering point against the lightening sky. "There aren't as many watchfires on this side."

"Bryn Tyddwl is a servient city. Servients don't like fire. Fire's Second Magic."

"I thought iron —"

"You can't have iron without fire. They go together. So do the sun and heat and deserts. They're all Second Magic."

"Then what's First Magic?"

"Night and the moon, water, earth, and stone. Green things, too." He shrugged. "Dead things, as well; it's all the same to the Circle."

They hurried on. Suddenly the bridge seemed to shiver. The great iron cables were grinding like teeth in a nightmare.

"What's happening?" Morgan asked, startled and afraid.

"Thermals," he said. "The firepit's heating up. It's almost dawn."

They both turned involuntarily. In the east the sky was a haze of angry red streaks. "We've got to get out of here right away," Arddu said. He took her wrist. They began to run. The western edge of the canyon was clearer now, a dark bulk outlined against the sky.

All at once Arddu jerked to a halt. Ahead of them were two small pyramids, copper-colored and faintly glowing, attached to the supports at each side of the walkway.

"What are they?" Morgan whispered, dry-mouthed.

"Alarms." He cursed under his breath. "They're Second Magic, can't you see? We'll never get past them."

Only a short distance beyond the pyramids was the end of the bridge. Morgan wanted to scream. Everything they'd been through, and now they weren't going to escape after all! Rage flooded her, an ice-cold torrent like a waterfall, electric. She threw back her head.

"Put on the torc," she ordered Arddu. The words came from deep within her. She sounded different even to herself, authority in her voice, a certainty more powerful than instinct.

Arddu blinked at her.

"Put it on!" she commanded. "It'll get you past."

He frowned in amazement, then without a word jerked the thick gold necklet from his cloak and jammed it around his neck. It was too big for him now, and out of shape, but it held. He grimaced.

"Go on," she said, still commanding.

"But how will you —?"

"You'll throw the torc back to me."

She watched him as he stepped forward into the danger area. A heartbeat later he was through. Except for a momentary fading of the glow surrounding the pyramids, there was no sign that any notice had been made of Arddu's passing.

"It worked," he breathed. "They thought I was a Linesman!" He took off the torc. "Get ready!"

71

She nodded. Quickly he tossed the torc down the walkway toward her. She caught it casually. Arddu frowned. It was as if Morgan had known there was no chance of the torc going astray into the canyon and leaving her stranded on the bridge forever.

It was only then, with the torc safe in her hands, that her assurance faded. She began to shake. A minute passed, and still she didn't move.

"Put it on," Arddu called. "Morgan, put it on!"

It wasn't iron, but it had been around a Linesman's neck. Sickness rose in her throat.

"Morgan! It's almost daylight!"

She took a deep breath, a second one, a third. The luck of threes, she thought. Gagging, she put on the torc. And stumbling and retching, she ran past the alarms to Arddu, then wrenched off the torc and tossed it backward, down into the canyon.

★

For a moment Arddu could only shake his head. Who was she, this girl who could change from panic to coolness and back again in the flicker of an eyelash? How had she known that the alarms would let them through if they wore the torc? And the way she had ordered him around, as arrogant and assured as Rigan herself! He had obeyed her almost without thinking, as if she were the expert and he the stranger on this world.

The sun was rising. They had to find a place to hide. He looked north up the iron road that cut around a heap of shale that separated them from the city of Bryn Tyddwl. There people would be awakening; Red Cloaks, too. And only the public wells for water, and this girl without even a cloak to cover her Circle looks and alien clothing.

He looked south. It was a broken land of stone and baked earth: pure desert, the kind of land that could mean death by thirst in a day. Nevertheless there might be a hiding place for them there. He took off his cloak and arranged it to cover both their heads. Then, with an arm around Morgan's shoulders, he headed south, looking for shelter.

She went with him unprotesting, like a tired child. From shadow to shadow they scurried, huddled under the brown safety of his cloak, while the sky grew bright. Arddu kept well away from the Ystavingon Road, but he knew they might still encounter people. Bryn Tyddwl was the trading center for all of east Eifionydd, and people would be traveling now, before it grew too hot.

They were about half a league south of the city when Morgan sank to her knees. Through the confusion in her mind he caught a few flashing images: a woman smiling cautiously, a gray island splashed by a colorless sea, a piece of glass framing a solitary curlew.

"Get up!" he ordered her.

"Can't . . . so tired . . ."

He dragged her upright. "You'll be more than tired if you don't keep moving!"

Somehow they trudged on. It was getting hotter, the arid wind drying their sweat almost before it could form. Arddu cursed silently, knowing he couldn't afford the moisture loss. It had been a long time since he had tasted water. Suddenly he gave a hoarse cry of gladness. In the heat-hazed flatness of the desert ahead was a place of stones.

He had to drag Morgan to the stones. Casting a hunted look at the whitening sky, he found a sharp piece of rock and began making a trench in the earth shaded by an enormous standing stone. Desperately he labored with his makeshift tool. The deeper he got, the more the leaning stone would shelter them. Morgan sat with her back against another stone, her head curved into her knees. He didn't tell her of the desert sun that could kill in an afternoon. There was no point.

After a time she began to help, piling up loosened earth beside the trench. They worked a little longer, but then Arddu stopped. The trench was just big enough for one.

"Get in," he ordered Morgan.

"What about you?"

"One of us has to go into the city for water. And with your looks you wouldn't get past the first servient."

"Your looks are just as —"

"I have a hood to hide under," he pointed out, "and Nwm is my world, not yours."

She stared at him, white as the sky. "You won't come back. You'll go away and leave me here."

"If you think that," he said, "you'd deserve it." And he turned his back on her and went away.

★

She took up Arddu's stone and labored away at the trench, making it big enough for two, though the sweat poured off her and she was half dead already with dehydration and fatigue. When Arddu came back, he would see what she had done, and know she had trusted him. When he came back . . .

But the day passed, and the stone dropped from her hands. She had no more tears. She had no more sweat. If Menw himself had come along she would have begged him for water. She was alone, caught in the sizzling struggle of sun and stone. And her tongue swelled, and her eyes puffed and closed, and she moved in and out of nightmare.

"And do you like your room, Miss Lefay?"

Gray islands, gray ghosts. Dad had made it look safe. He had made her want to be there.

A green jade horseshoe whose luck had gone bad. Maybe if she hadn't put the horseshoe into her jeans pocket, she wouldn't have gone over to Tintagel in the first place.

Lake Ontario. Waves beating on the shore under a sleeting rain. Cold, fresh water. Water!

She had gone over to Tintagel. Nobody had made her. She'd gone to meet her father; and then someone had held her hand and pulled her, because the M'rlendd was waiting. And then there had been a baby to look after. And from then on, always, the M'rlendd waiting to take over for the Line.

Arddu, please come back. Mom, oh, Mom!

"They're all the same, Morgan. Don't let them fool you. You can't trust them. They'll make you believe in them and then they'll disappoint you."

Please, Arddu, please don't make me be alone!

Then hands took her up and pried her puffed and greedy lips apart, and water poured in, lovely, lovely water; and she drank until she could drink no more, and then she slept.

PART II

Arthur was crying, a thing neither she nor the M'rlendd liked, though for different reasons. The Morrigan rocked him briefly, then wiped away the blood on his knee and briskly put him down. "So many tears for this little blood?" she asked, shaking her head. First Magic wasted, she thought, wasted with every teardrop. He was four years old; why couldn't he understand? "Come," she commanded, getting to her feet and heading for the door. Sniffing and burbling, he followed.

She spent as little time in the hut as she could. It drained her. There was too much iron in it, too many straight lines. The M'rlendd had built it, of course. He had built his hut where he could gloat at the First Magic sea, and there he stayed.

Of all things, that worried the Morrigan. The M'rlendd, surrounded by the sound of water, had made himself at home here, had made his magic adapt. She had heard that this was a characteristic of Second Magic. It was not fixed to the old ways. It was even prepared to experiment to make itself more powerful.

This was the first time she had realized what a strength it was.

She took the sea path, the one that led to the western over-look. It was almost sunfall, and even on this world sunfall was a sight to cause rejoicing. Arthur ran after her, struggling to keep up. She ignored him, but kept a wary eye out for the M'rlendd. A short while before, she had seen him heading for

76

the other side of the island, but with him you never knew. He was probably going to his cave. His cave! That was another blasphemy, even more than the hut overlooking the sea. The womb of the Mother had become a place of Second Magic.

She had followed him there once, her anger driving her, but with Arthur and all her plans at stake there had been nothing she could do. His firepot had cast its bloody glow on the walls of a place that until him had known only darkness. And there, inside the bones of the Mother, he had mixed his chemicals and smelted his iron and she had done nothing to stop him. Then the M'rlendd had turned and smiled at her and asked her if she had come to learn from him! It was at times like this that the Morrigan wondered how much she had deceived him.

A storm was coming in. From the overlook, a flattened stone with a dizzying drop to the rocks below, the Morrigan saw the rain coming, great sheets of it sweeping over the sea. Her breath caught. She could feel her magic straining at the bonds she had placed on it. Her time was at night, but it had to be a night with a moon — and that would not be tonight. In reaction she turned to Arthur. Lifting him by both hands, she swung him out over the precipice, observing his pleasure in the game, his confidence in her.

"Whom do you love?" she asked him softly, a ritual.

"The Mother," he answered happily. "You."

"Whom do you obey?"

"Whom I must."

"Whom do you hide from?"

"The M'rlendd." And he laughed, spoiling it. "And you, too, sometimes, Morgan! You couldn't find me when I hid in the grain pit today, could you?"

A game, that was all it was to him. Well, he was young; he would learn. The Morrigan placed his small body carefully beside her on the overlook, her arm going around him as a matter of course. Ah, but these young ones, how they needed love!

The rain hit them then, cold and soaking and full of the power of the Mother. "Let's go home!" Arthur said. "Morgan, I'm wet! Let's go home!"

Yes, he was still very, very young.

EIGHT

May I not fall into the embrace of the swamp,
Into the mob that peoples the depths of Uffern.
I greatly fear the flinty covering
With the Guledig of the boundless country.
    — Book of Taliessin, LII
        (The Praise of Lludd the Great)

W HEN Morgan awoke, she was still in the trench by the standing stone, and Arddu was asleep beside her in the space she had made for him. It was getting dark. It was also much cooler, cool enough for her to need the extra cloak he had spread over her shoulders. She huddled into it, looking up at the moon, waiting for him to awake.

Her thoughts were soft with gratitude, hardly a whisper in his mind, but they woke Arddu. Embarrassed, he sat up, wrapping his cloak around him.

"I'm sorry I took so long," he said.

She looked away. "I didn't deserve for you to come back at all. You said so yourself."

He held out a water-pouch. "Are you thirsty?"

She was, very, but she took only a few sips. "It's all right," he said, noticing how careful she was being. "We can get more tonight."

"Where did you get it?"

"The water pouch? The market. I got your cloak there, too. We had to have something to cover that hair of yours."

"I hope you found something to eat, while you were at it."

He reached into a bag he'd stashed beside him and handed her a squashed, dried-out hunk of bread and some leathery meat. She shared it with him, and then they both drank again.

After a moment she asked tentatively, "Arddu, what happens now? We can't just stay here forever. The Line is sure to find us."

"Unless we can get out of the east, the Line will find us wherever we go. And west is the Circle, which is almost as bad."

"Is it really?"

He nodded grimly.

She bit her lip. "At least the Circle doesn't like the Line. That's one thing in their favor. Couldn't we —"

"The Circle doesn't like me, either, and it won't like you. We both look too much like Sisters."

"What's wrong with that?"

"Everything, unless you happen to be a female with First Magic," he said. "You've got about as much chance of the Sisters agreeing to send you home as —"

"Could they send me home?" Her voice was suddenly breathless.

"Of course they *could*. But they wouldn't."

"Is there any other way for me to get back to Earth?"

Reluctantly he said, "Only the Circle and the Line do missionings."

She leaned forward, looking into his face. Her eyes were desperate. "Earth is my home, Arddu! How would you feel if you had a home you could never go back to?"

His hands gripped one another tightly. He didn't answer.

"You said it yourself. Everything on Nwm belongs to either the Circle or the Line. If we end up with the Line, we're dead. But if we could tell the Circle what's happened and ask for their help —"

"Listen to me, Morgan! The Circle won't help you. Even if it would, we're easily three hundred leagues from Gorseth Arberth."

"It's someplace to aim for, at least!"

"You aren't listening. Gorseth Arberth is an island. There's only one ship that takes outsiders there. And the Circle has banished me, so that ship wouldn't take us, even if we could get to it. And I don't even know how we'd cross the desert!"

"You managed it in the other direction, didn't you?"

"Only because the Line wanted me to. I came by windsled. You and I can't do that."

"What's a windsled?"

"It's a kind of land ship. Line servients sail them across Eifionydd."

"Over sand?"

"No, there are roads. Iron, of course."

Morgan was thinking hard. "The Line believes I'm the Morrigan. She wouldn't go anywhere near iron. So if we went there. . . . And there's always someplace to hide on a ship. A cargo area. Something."

"Hide," he repeated, staring at her. "Four days at least. No weapons. A crew of five or six checking things out every day. Nothing to eat and only one water pouch between us. Anyway, Menw knows you're not really Rigan. He'll make up some reason to watch the roads."

"It's better than staying here!"

Arddu rolled over on his side, turning his face right away from her. He was silent for so long that Morgan wondered if he had gone back to sleep. At last he turned over again. "You're right," he said. "Dead is dead, however you look at it. It might as well be on a windsled as anywhere else."

★

Even from a distance and at night, Bryn Tyddwl made Morgan uneasy. The smell alone was daunting, the stink of refuse and old excesses wafting out onto the plain. As they got nearer, the city became nastier still, the buildings jammed together like an entrenched army. It seemed less a city than an animal waiting out the night.

They kept to the plain as long as possible, circling the city from the southwest. When they got to a steep ravine Arddu remembered, he led Morgan into the city, aiming for the public well he'd discovered that morning. He seemed to know exactly where he was going. Morgan envied him both his night sight and his sense of direction. She herself felt completely lost only a few minutes after passing through the first of the clay-baked shacks.

As Arddu had predicted, there was no one outside. There was garbage and the sound of people talking and a stink like toilets and now and then a watchfire, but no visible people at all. Morgan kept as close to Arddu as she could. She had never seen such streets in her life. Paths unraveled like wool in a cat's paw, little threads running off in all directions, then joining again in furry tangles, hopelessly confusing. Some were barely wide enough to drive a goat, and stank of dung and old cooking. Arddu seemed to prefer these, avoiding the wider, more inviting ways.

All of the houses were made of clay bricks, and all had doors and windows, but none were open. The windows were curtained with what seemed to be animal skins, only half-tanned, by the smell of them. In places there were thick, putrefying puddles beneath the windows, which Morgan told herself she'd die rather than walk through. Cracks of light showed where the curtains didn't quite fit. Behind the curtains Morgan could hear the clink of cutlery, the yowling of cats and babies, the grunts of people brawling, the flutter of pigeons. She and Arddu passed like ghosts through it all. No one noticed them. The whole of Bryn Tyddwl seemed battened down against the night.

At last they came to a junction, a small, open area where several paths met. There was a well in the middle. Surrounding it was a triangular iron path on which burning firepots had been placed. After the darkness in the rest of the city, the brightness made Morgan squint. They paused in a shadow at the edge of the courtyard. Arddu was frowning.

"Are you sure it's the same well?" Morgan whispered. "You didn't say anything about firepots."

"There weren't any this morning." He gnawed his thumbnail. "Maybe they're always lit at night, though, so that people can find their way to the wells."

"But you said no one ever goes out at night."

"Unless they have to." He seemed to be trying to convince himself. "I was safe enough this morning. And we have to have water. What I brought back this afternoon is almost gone."

81

"If you were Menw," Morgan said, "and you had two prisoners that had been gone a whole day in the boiling sun without water, wouldn't you guard the wells at night?"

"Maybe we can find a well without firepots," Arddu said at last. "We can look for one on our way to the windport."

Keeping to the flickering shadows at the edge of the courtyard, they took the first new path they came to. It was one of the wider ones, and it led northward toward the windport. As they hurried on, the city quietened. All over Bryn Tyddwl, behind the thousands of sweating, stinking curtains, the lights were going out. It was lonely without the thin cracks of light. Arddu was relieved by it, though; Morgan could tell by the quickening of his footsteps. They didn't speak, and their soft shoes made only whispers against the ground. But now and then a dog barked sharply, and Arddu grew worried.

"Richer street," he muttered. "More dogs."

He took a turning shortly after that, choosing a mean little alley that he seemed to think went in the right direction. Morgan had stopped wondering how he could tell; she just followed him. She looked up, but here even the moon was invisible, obscured by a heap of taller hovels. The stars she could see were very bright; they made her feel more lonely than ever.

Night deepened. At the end of a path branching to their left, Morgan saw another public well: not as big an open area as before, but just as brightly lit. Arddu said nothing, and they passed the junction. Their little path narrowed, a nerve ending of an alley that made even single file a squeeze. Another one joined it a little farther on.

Just before they got there, Arddu stopped so abruptly that Morgan bumped into him. His hands went backward into her chest, warning her not to make a sound. Still as shadows, they waited. Someone moved on the other path: a hulking dark figure that suddenly split into two.

A voice cursed softly. "We've been waiting here all night, and nothing."

"What did you think was going to happen?" sneered the other. "That First Magic witch is leagues away by this time. We're on a fool's errand, as usual."

"Gods burn all Linesmen." A mournful mutter from the first man.

Gently Arddu's hand pushed backward. Morgan slid one foot behind her, then another.

"The firepots would have been enough. Why they needed us, too —"

Quietly, quietly, Morgan and Arddu made their way backward. Now they had reached the branching that led to the second well. It was slightly wider here, and Arddu maneuvered himself to face her. He jerked his head to the right. Somehow Morgan knew what he meant. They would take the next path to the right. But there was no room for him to get in front of her. Blindly she turned around. I'm in the lead, she thought. I can hardly see, and I'm in the lead. And those men will hear if I bump into anything.

Slowly, she began to move. Her arms were out like a sleepwalker's. Don't let a dog bark, she prayed. She found that she was breathing in bursts, desperate little gasps of air followed by long seconds of holding her breath. Behind them, little by little, the voices faded.

They came to a path. She would have missed it, but Arddu plucked at her sleeve, and she stopped. There was just room for him to squeeze by her. He headed right down the path, and now that he was in the lead, it was easier. But she kept imagining the men were just behind her. A long time passed. Arddu took another turning, and shortly afterward, another. There were no longer any voices in the night.

They passed another firepot-studded courtyard with a third well. It reminded Morgan how thirsty she was. But there were only a few mouthfuls left in their water pouch. Her stomach ached with nervousness. They had to have water. Their whole plan depended on it. If she and Arddu couldn't use the public wells, what were they going to do?

A short distance beyond the courtyard, Arddu stopped. With his lips to her ear, he said, "There'll be water supplies in the huts. People don't go out at night, and they have to have water."

"We're going to break in?"

"I am. You're going to wait outside."

"Here?" she whispered, nervously jamming her hands into the pockets of her jeans. Her left hand closed on something cool and oddly familiar. It was her lucky horseshoe. She had forgotten she even had it with her.

Suddenly, it seemed to quicken. Hardly knowing what she was doing, she pulled it from her pocket and held it up, just as they turned a corner.

Here, the moon was visible. It shone on the little horseshoe, turning it into something bright and large and no longer green. It was white as the moon, white as a seabird's flight, white as winter's first snow. Without letting herself think, she made a wish. Arddu whirled, seeing the horseshoe like a light in her fingers. And then the horseshoe faded and became ordinary again, and Morgan put it back into her pocket.

"Where —" Arddu got out, a strangled sound, then began again. "How did you get that?"

"My grandmother gave it to me. Here," she whispered, pointing to the cracked wall of the hovel to their left. "There's water inside. You can get it. You won't get caught." He looked at her. Expressions chased each other over his face: uncertainty, suspicion, hope, regret. "Quick," she insisted, "through the window."

He didn't say a word, just did her bidding. And she stood outside and waited, knowing there would be no alarm, knowing he would bring back a full water pouch. And the strangest part was, it all seemed the most natural thing in the world.

★

"You wasted it," he said when they were far away, the water pouch heavy in his hand. "Three wishes, that's all the Made Magics give you, and you wasted one of them on that."

She was silent, disconcerted. So she hadn't known, he thought. She possessed something that could only have been made by the Circle itself, and she hadn't known. Yet she had known how to use it. Voicelessly, suspiciously, he regarded her. But the moon was lost behind a hill, and she was as formless as the night. Her thoughts were dim, too, like voices whispering. He couldn't understand her.

He turned away. "Don't use it again," he said then, over his shoulder, "not unless you have to. And whatever you do, don't try to use it near fire or iron."

The end of the city came as a surprise. One minute they were surrounded by houses, and the next they were on a hilltop overlooking the market. It lay on the edge of the moon-lit desert that stretched west and north as far as they could see. It was very windy, their hoods blowing back, their hair scattering and blending like silver threads. The ground ahead was a fabric of living light, the darkness easing and shifting constantly with the whirling moon. Wordlessly, Arddu indicated the way down.

In the market they crept unobserved past lines of open stalls hung with tapestries. There was strange lettering on some of the tapestries, signs announcing food for trade, clothing exchanges, and leather stalls. With a start, Morgan realized that she was reading a foreign language.

"I can read those signs," she whispered agitatedly, pulling Arddu to a halt. "How can I —?"

"You *speak* the language," he whispered back. "Why wouldn't you read it?"

She stared at him. Of course she spoke the language. She'd been talking to him since the beginning.

"Maybe it's something to do with your summoning," Arddu said. "People can't be sent to new worlds without knowing how to talk. Now will you please keep quiet and come on?"

Hurt, Morgan drew away from him. He took her arm impatiently, and she was disturbed to find herself grateful. She was so dependent on him! They walked in silence until they were out of the bazaar and into an open area crisscrossed by the clay walls of animal pens. Horses and oxen snuffled and stomped dully, uninterested in the two brown cloaks hurrying by. The white smoke of their breath rose and was lost in the cold desert wind. The stench was terrible. Animals had to be very badly cared for, Morgan thought, to smell like this.

"No one in the east wastes cleaning water on slaughter beasts," Arddu said. She didn't notice that he had answered her thoughts.

85

They were still some distance east of the windport, but ahead of them was a tent city where Arddu said the crews of the windsleds slept when they were in port. The windsleds brought the animals east from Circle lands that ate no red meat, and as well they brought grains and gold and fire opals. Flint and marble and silver went west to pay for it all.

"The food all comes from Circle lands? Are you telling me the Line would starve without the windsleds, and the Circle still keeps trading with them? I thought the Circle hated Linesmen!"

"It would mean open war for the Circle to cut off trade with the windsleds. Anyway, trade is good for the Circle, too. There are things the Sisters need for their magics that can be found only in Line territory."

"Like what?" she asked.

"Like that jade of yours. And there are always a few windsleds willing to risk the chasm to get it to them."

"Is jade illegal, then?"

"In the east," Arddu said drily, "a cargo of jade is more illegal than murder."

They went on, giving the tent city wide berth. At last the windport came into view. Metal walkways like docks gleamed in the moonlight. Tied to them were the windsleds, looking to Morgan like anchored catamarans. Through the rush of the wind she could hear their metal masts jangling. For a searing moment she thought of Toronto harbor, its yachts with their colorful flags, the windsurfers, the ferry that went back and forth to Toronto Island in the dappled light of summer. But this was another world. In this world ships sailed on iron roads instead of water. In this world bitter enemies provided one another with the necessities of life.

It took longer than they wanted to reach the docks. There were perhaps fifty windsleds in harbor, enormous twin-keeled ships with holds like moving vans and rope ladders hanging over the sides.

"Which one?" Morgan asked Arddu.

"It'll have to be one whose holds are just about full," he replied, "or the crew might be waiting for new shipments."

"But if the holds are full, where'll we hide? And what if we choose a windsled that's heading for Uffern?"

"I don't know," he said. "This is your plan, remember?"

"Can you think of another one?"

"It's too late to start thinking. The sun will be up soon, and there's nowhere on this side of the city to hide."

So it was a windsled or nothing. Morgan took a deep breath. "We'd better start looking," she said.

NINE

This leaf, is it not driven by the wind?
Woe to it as to its fate!
It is old, this year was it born.
     — Red Book of Hergest XI

S HE didn't make a wish. She didn't dare let herself even
   reach into the pocket where the horseshoe was. They had
gotten out of the canyon and survived a whole day in the
desert on their own, she reminded herself. But windsled after
windsled was wrong for them, either too full or too empty,
and once, frighteningly, full of the windsled's crew, snoring
in ragged blankets on the deck. Morgan and Arddu got out
without waking anyone, but Morgan's heart was pounding so
loudly she could hardly hear the wind.

In the east the sky was paling. She looked at it in despair.
Night was almost over. There were only five windsleds left
on this dock, and time to check out maybe one of them. She
ran after Arddu to the next windsled in line.

"It's got to be this one," Arddu muttered, reaching for the
rope ladder. She clambered up after him, praying that he was
right.

She didn't like it at all. The first hold had no decking, and
it was full of live animals: pale-skinned calves with hopeless
eyes, frantic birds whose feathers were ragged from their wire
cages, rodents skittering madly among heaps of droppings.
The cages were stacked amid piles of hides. Even in the wind
everything stank with rot and excrement and the sharp odor
of tanning fluid. Arddu ploughed grimly ahead, aiming for the
hold in the second keel.

That had a partial deck in the stern, housing the steering apparatus and a lot of cables. A metal companionway led down to an area too black to see into. Arddu led the way to the open front part of the hold. There he began prying at the lids of some crates packed into the hull.

"What're you doing?" Morgan asked him nervously.

"Looking for a place to hide." His face was pinched with exhaustion.

"But you said livestock went from west to east. And we want to go the other way!"

"There's no time to find another windsled." He jerked his head at the brightening sky. "Anyway, maybe this one isn't leaving right away. If we could stay here just for today . . ."

He got one of the lids open. It was packed to the brim with rough-cut ore. "Maybe we could dump this somewhere. Then there'd be room for us."

He began lifting some out. Morgan helped. Suddenly they came on a different layer, dark green and shining translucently. Arddu's breath whooshed out. "Jade!" he exclaimed. "This windsled must be going west after all!"

"Why?"

"Because jade's First Magic. That's why it's illegal for Line servients to trade it. Only the Circle would want it."

"What are those animals doing here, if this ship is going west?"

"Someone wants the Line to think it's going east. Maybe westbound ships are searched, who knows?" He began thinking aloud. "The roads only go to a few ports near enough to the Circle to allow for direct trading. . . ." He paused, then nodded. "Awarnach," he said, with satisfaction. "It's a Line city, but it's just across the River Ffraw from Tren. And Tren's a Circle city, and wealthy. And, Morgan, Awarnach's only about forty leagues from the sea. We could cover that on foot in four or five days."

"I don't care where we're going, as long as it isn't east." She bit her lip, thinking hard. "But we'd better not hide in a crate. They're bound to watch the jade pretty carefully."

"There's no other hiding place on this side," Arddu said.

"What about under that deck back there?"

"That's the crew's quarters."

Which left the other side, Morgan thought. Her stomach turned. The stench was bad enough over here, but at close quarters in the desert sun, the other hold would be revolting.

In the growing light the wind strengthened suddenly. "We haven't much time," Arddu said, piling ore back into the crate he had opened.

She helped him fasten it shut again. Then they pulled themselves up to the bridge that linked the two hulls of the catamaran. At once they ducked down, for there were people coming out of the tent city toward the docks. An enormous woman led the way, with six or seven men and women behind her.

"They're coming here!" Arddu whispered. He pulled Morgan off the bridge and into the other hold. Frantically they began searching the mess of live and dead animals for someplace to hide.

"There!"

Arddu was pointing to a large stack of fodder in the bow. They didn't have time to consider it carefully. Voices were already sounding at the foot of the ladder outside. Like scuttling mice they leaped for the straw, helping each other, heaping hay over feet and legs, bodies, heads and arms. *Slosh, slosh, slosh.* The water-pouch, Morgan thought; couldn't Arddu keep it quiet?

A woman's voice roared from the other hold. "Sun's up, and you're still lazing! You, Llawr! Take Gwal and get that mainsail up. Erfddyl, check below. Doged, you stand by to cast us off, and if you see any Red Cloaks coming, you just turn blind and deaf. The rest of you to the cleats. We're getting out of here!"

★

No one investigated the haystack trembling in the bow. No one even came near. Morgan and Arddu could see nothing, but they could hear: the mainsail rising, the flap of the foresail, the captain's shouts, the squeak of blocks. Then with a tug and a jerk they were sailing. Flap! Flap! The desert wind caught them at an angle. They veered sideways.

"Closer to the wind!" they heard dimly. "Pull up! Away from the edge!" This last was even more muffled, almost lost in the hiss and whine of six pairs of wheels on the iron road, and the ever-present whistle of the wind.

Day grew, a white ceiling blistering with heat. The haystack was protected from the wind and the sun by an overhang in the bows, but it was not an ideal hiding place. It was itchy and hot despite the wild wind sucking the windsled forward. As the day wore on, Morgan and Arddu had to exert real effort just to breathe. The straw seemed turned to needles, but they tried not to stir in case the stack slipped and revealed them. For a long time they wouldn't even drink. But as the heat intensified, the water-pouch went back and forth, while the hay shifted alarmingly. No one in the other hull noticed. They were lulled after that, made lazy with heat and tiredness; and they dozed, and drank, and dozed again, deep in their cocoon of straw, until the sun was low in the west, and hunger brought them to life.

They had nothing to eat. "We'll try for something later," Arddu muttered, "when it gets dark."

Morgan's stomach rumbled. She had lost track of the last time she had eaten a real meal. "Will they sail all night?" she asked.

"Traders usually do," Arddu said. "They don't like the night, but speed's important for perishables."

"And for illegal cargoes like jade," Morgan pointed out.

Arddu grunted. "The captain was worried about Red Cloaks. If the Line has even an inkling what this sled is carrying . . ."

"You mean the jade, or us?"

"Either," he said gloomily.

"But the Line can't stop a windsled, can it?"

"It'd be easier just to send word to the next port to have us searched when we get there. Messenger hawks are faster than windsleds."

The sun sank lower, dragging the heat with it. The windsled sailed more quietly, the wind changing with the onset of evening. Morgan wasn't hungry anymore. She just felt sick.

"What if the Line has sent a hawk?" she asked after a long time. "Could we get off this sled before we got to port?"

91

"We're going fairly fast. It'd be dangerous."

"It would be more dangerous to wait for the Line to dig us out of here."

"I know," Arddu said. He shrugged, and the hay shifted a little. "We'll go slower when it's dark. Maybe we could manage jumping off tomorrow night. By then the worst of the desert should be past."

Tomorrow night, Morgan thought. A whole day away. On this world that seemed an eternity.

Arddu seemed to sense her disquietude, and for a long time after that he talked about other things. He told Morgan about the two domains of Nwm: the desert of the east, where only the Line went, and the swamps and farms and oceans of the west that was Encircled. As for the south, he said, it was divided, a varied land whose allegiance shifted with the seasons. In winter it sided with the Circle, in summer with the Line. To Morgan it seemed a crazy system. Thinking about that, she didn't notice that he hadn't mentioned the north.

He spoke then of First and Second Magic, and how they had taken over from the solitary old magic that had existed on Nwm before them. "First Magic was the most important for a long time," he said, "but then Second got stronger, and it's been getting more powerful ever since." And he explained how, once Nwm had been portioned out, the two Magics had expanded across time and space, seeking new worlds for Alignment or Encircling.

"So that was why Rigan was sent to Earth!" Morgan said. "But how would she go about trying to — Encircle — it?"

"The Magics have a way of knowing the people who are going to be important in the history of a world. Maybe all Rigan would have to do is influence just the one right person."

"Who would then hand over a whole world?" Morgan shook her head in disbelief. "Would the Line have sent someone to Earth, too?"

"Rigan told me a Linesman named the M'rlendd would be her enemy on Earth."

"The M'rlendd!" she exclaimed. "But that was the name of the man I saw! It was one of those dreams I told you about

92

— a really early Tintagel, and the M'rlendd waiting, and the girl going to meet him, but hating him —"

"The girl?" Arddu asked, breathing too fast. He'd been wanting to ask her about this for a long time, but there'd been no way, short of admitting he could read her mind.

Morgan moved uncomfortably. "The one I kept dreaming about. You know, the one who looked like — us."

"She was Rigan," Arddu said, jumping at it. "She must have been. She had our looks, and the M'rlendd was her enemy—"

"But she had brown hair, not blond like us."

"Hair can be dyed."

"Why would I dream about your sister when I didn't even know she existed?"

"Why do you look like her at all?"

"Lots of people have doubles. You've got Rigan."

"Rigan and I are in the same family. What about you?"

Silence.

"All right," he said, a bit louder. "How is it that you happen to possess a Made Magic from Nwm?"

"The horseshoe, you mean? I told you, it's been passed down through our family, but only to the women in it."

"*Somebody* must have had it first. Morgan, listen. Before Rigan was missioned, she was given a Made Magic. It was a circlet made of jade, and she was supposed to take it to Earth."

"Mine isn't a circlet," Morgan said stubbornly. "It's a horseshoe."

"Half of a circle, you mean. Maybe the original circlet was broken, and your family only got one of the halves. Morgan, your dream shows that Rigan went back to Earth's ancient times. You have her looks. You have a Made Magic from Nwm. It came down to you through your family line. What in the name of the Mother can you be, except Rigan's direct descendant?"

She went very still.

"Well?" he demanded frustratedly.

"I'm going to sleep," she said.

"You can't! We're talking about —"

"We're talking about your *sister*," Morgan lashed out. "Your *twin;* the same age as you! You're saying she was my great-

93

great-great-grandmother — or even older. Do you honestly expect me to believe that you're that old?"

"I'm not," he said. "But Rigan might be. Time doesn't run the same in different worlds. If Rigan was missioned to Earth's past, twenty nights might pass for her like twenty years, or even —"

"Twenty centuries would be more like it. Don't you see? If it's all true, Rigan died centuries ago. She's dead of old age, Arddu, and you're still only a kid!"

And Arddu, dumbstruck, could not say a word.

TEN

Let us not reproach one another,
but rather mutually save ourselves.
— Black Book of Caermarthen VII

IN the middle of the night, when the moon ruled the sky, they crawled quietly out of the haystack to look for food. Over in the other hull, only the helmsman was audibly awake. Morgan could hear him whistling tunelessly, the kind of song some people use to keep unpleasant thoughts at bay. It was cool, though the wind was fitful. The flap of the sails and the creak of the steering gear were ghosts of their daytime selves. Morgan shivered into her cloak and crept after Arddu, whose eyes were so much better in moonlight, and who actually seemed to believe they would find something to satisfy their gnawing hunger. She did not. She didn't think they would find anything, when the animals were so badly neglected.

She supposed she ought to be glad that no one had cleaned the cages or fed the poor beasts, for there was little doubt that was what the haystack had been intended for. But it was hard to be grateful in the face of such misery. The calves, especially: it wrenched her heart to see their huge, tired eyes lifting to her face, expecting nothing, not even hoping. They had been only a cover for the curious of Bryn Tyddwl, and now that the city was behind them, no one cared if they lived or died.

She made her way back to the haystack for some fodder and shoved it between the bars. The animals didn't even sniff at it. She went to the water barrel and filled a gourd, pouring it into each water trough. "Here," she whispered to the first calf, a bony-nosed thing that seemed all legs, "have a drink.

95

Go on, drink!" A fierce joy went through her as the little animal nosed the trough, then began to drink. Another followed, and another. From cage to cage she went, while Arddu shook his head at the futility of her actions — though it was what Rigan would have done, what any of the Circle would have done. He himself had enough to do to find food humans could eat.

He searched everywhere he could think of, even the bird cages, looking for eggs. He found a stack of dried and untanned animal skins, some with a little meat on them. The Circle did not eat meat, and this was foul-smelling and unappetizing, but he scraped it off anyway. The time might come when he and Morgan would not be particular about what they ate. Morgan joined him then, helping him search, lifting the lids of crates and soundlessly replacing them, opening sail lockers, going through the pockets of someone's abandoned vest. The darkness was thinning when they finished. The results were disappointing: a single raw egg, a small bag of bird seed, a few pieces of ancient jerky that the martens had mauled and left, and Arddu's meat scrapings. They didn't dare go into the other hull, where the real food would be. Miserably they refilled their water skin at the barrel and went back to their haystack. Hungry as they were, it was a long time before they could make themselves eat.

★

Morgan yawned. "It's not nearly so hot today, is it?" She yawned again, her jaw cracking. She longed to be able to stretch.

"We've come a long way," Arddu said. "This sled must go faster than I thought." His voice was tense.

All day Arddu had seemed uneasy. Over and over, against all reason, he would shove aside the straw that covered their faces and stare up at the small patch of sky visible beyond the overhang. The first time, they had seen a bird, floating high and effortless, pacing the windsled with a few lazy flaps of its wings. It almost seemed as if it wanted to stay with them. Arddu had stared at it silently. Seeing his face, Morgan decided not to say anything. Later, they saw it again, or another just like it; and later still, and again. Morgan had finally refused to look anymore.

"Do you think we'll get to Awarnach before nightfall?" she asked now.

"I hope not. I want us to be gone from this sled long before it reaches port. Those hawks . . ."

He didn't have to say more. Clearly he believed Red Cloaks, or worse, would be waiting for the sled when it reached port.

"Could we try jumping off the sled now?" she asked nervously. "The wind's not quite so strong. If we hung from the ladder, we wouldn't have far to fall."

"And I suppose the crew will conveniently turn blind while we're doing it?" Arddu said sarcastically.

"I have my horseshoe. Couldn't I wish —?"

"We're on an iron road," he reminded her. "First Magic doesn't work here." He brushed impatiently at the straw over his face. "Gods, I wish I could see!"

To Morgan's distress, he half sat up. The haystack, already much mistreated, began to topple. Desperately they clutched at it, but it was too late. Faster the hay slid, and faster. Then suddenly, over in the other hull, they heard what they had been dreading for two days.

"There's something in that haystack! Efrddyl, Doged! Get over there and see!"

★

After two days of inactivity they were too stiff to run. There was nowhere to go, anyway. Helpless and furious, they let themselves be taken. The two large men who dragged them out were businesslike about it, wasting no time talking, just hauling them like a catch of fish over the bridge. At last they were in front of the captain, the two men gripping their wrists behind their backs. For a moment no one said anything. Then the captain jerked off their hoods.

In the dusky light their hair gleamed palely. The men let go of their wrists and jumped back, cursing and drawing their knives. Even their captain whitened.

"Circle-spawn!" she spat, and made a strange gesture, the fat forefinger of her right hand cutting in half a circle made

97

with the thumb and forefinger of her left. Brown, piggy eyes glinted at them out of her rolls of fat. She had dark, thick eyebrows, and above them a line of glistening sweat. Her hair was sparse and greasy on a skull that seemed too small for her neck. Her brown cloak was filthy, and billowed like one of the sails on the windsled. She wore copper bracelets on each wrist, dozens of them, right up to her elbows.

"You're the ones the Red Cloaks were looking for," she said harshly, speaking through the broken circle she had made with her hands.

Two men, younger than the captain and thinner, but with the same piggy eyes, ranged themselves on either side of her, sharp blades at the ready.

"They're still looking," Arddu said, "if those hawks we've had with us all day are any indication."

The captain's eyes turned involuntarily skyward, but there were no birds there now, only the red streaks of approaching sunfall. Sweat dripped into the dirty tunic under her cloak. "They're not there now," she said. "No gods-burnt spies to see what we do to you." She jabbed the broken circle of her hands at Arddu's face.

"Put down your hands!" Arddu ordered her imperiously. "You are no Linesman, and *we* are not First Magic!"

The woman was a Line servient, and her masters were male. There was an authority in Arddu's voice that she had been taught to obey. Slowly her hands dropped to her sides. In the soft hiss of the crew's released breath, her voice sounded again, rough with defiance. "You're on a Line sled, on an iron road, and it's still daylight."

"We were in the Line's stronghold beside the fires of the chasm when we killed the Sdhe," Arddu said, calm and cold. He ignored Morgan's little movement of protest.

"Without magic you killed a Line-End?" The captain's voice was scornful.

"I did not say it was without magic."

"Not First Magic, you said, and anyone can see you're not Second! Bleached skin and fish eyes. Huh!"

"Look at me, Captain. I am a male, yet I have Circle looks. Has it been forgotten in the east that there was a time when

Nwm was united under a magic that was neither First Magic nor Second, but a union of both?"

The captain's eyes darted from Arddu to Morgan and back again. For an uneasy moment she was silent. "If you do have the old powers," she said at last, "why didn't you just sprout wings and fly to Awarnach instead of stowing away on our ship? Why don't you save your lives and do it now?"

"No magic can do everything," Arddu said. "But you will not kill us, because only we can get you safely into Awarnach with your cargo of jade."

The woman's breath whooshed out. Arddu pressed his advantage. "Those hawks prove the Line is suspicious of you. Whether your new Line-End thinks it is us you have on board or the jade, Red Cloaks will search your ship the moment you reach Awarnach. You can't turn back without arousing even more suspicion. You can't dump the jade because it would take too long to hide it, and the hawks would find anything that isn't hidden. You are doomed, Captain, unless you let us help you."

The woman wiped ineffectually at the greasy sweat dripping down her cheeks. "Why would you help us — supposing you really can?"

We have our own reasons for wanting to arrive undetected in Awarnach," Arddu said. "With the right materials, our magic could make that happen."

The captain gnawed her rubbery lips. "Prove it," she said at last. "Prove you have some kind of — Third Magic."

Morgan hunched miserably. She had been waiting for this. Prove Arddu's wild claim, when the only bit of magic she and Arddu possessed was a First Magic horseshoe that she couldn't even use here?

"If we made water spring up on your iron road," Arddu said, "would that be proof enough? Second Magic and First united, would that convince you? All we need is some of that flint by the road."

"Nobody on my ship touches that First Magic filth!"

"If we're going to produce water from iron," Arddu reminded her, "somebody will have to get that flint."

The captain looked up into the reddening sky. Then, suddenly, she made up her mind. "Keep an eye out for birds," she ordered two of the crew. "Helm into the wind. Pull up, I said!"

They turned abruptly, sails flapping. They coasted, slower, slower. The edge of the road was near. "Chocks!" one of the women shrilled. Someone went down the ladder, and the windsled shuddered to a stop.

"All right, you, down on the road," the captain said harshly to Morgan. "You'll be getting that stone. Your partner will stay here. He'll have six knives on him the moment you're off the iron, so don't try anything stupid."

Off the iron. Morgan looked swiftly at Arddu. Off the iron, where the jade horseshoe would work? Was all that business about a magic that was neither Second nor First just a trick to provide her a chance to use the horseshoe for a real wish?

"Go with her, Doged," the captain said. "Don't take your blade off her for a moment."

Doged's knife prodded Morgan, steering her to the side of the road. Under her cloak her trembling hand slid into her jeans pocket. Two wishes left, only two. Use it here, and there would be only one.

Use it wrong, and they would both be handed over to the Line.

"Here," growled Doged, jabbing her with the point of his knife, pointing to a heap of flinty stone. They were off the road. The only iron nearby was in his hand. Morgan took her hands out of her pocket and bent over, momentarily out of reach of the knife. He thought she was going to pick up the stone, but the horseshoe was in her hand. She looked under his outstretched arm to the moon, bright and mad in the northern sky.

And then she made a wish.

★

"I don't know why you couldn't have wished for us to be taken right to Gorseth Arberth," Arddu growled. "Even the river would have been better than here."

100

"This is a horseshoe," Morgan said defensively, "not a magic carpet. If I could have used it to get us somewhere, don't you think I'd already be back on Earth?"

They were standing in dry scrubland watching the wind-sled, sails reddened with sunfall, disappear into the north. Morgan had wished themselves forgotten. If Arddu had been in a better humor it might have been funny hearing the captain screeching about the unnecessary halt, nobody remembering that it had been her orders, nobody seeing him and Morgan standing there listening. But he couldn't forget those hawks. At best he and Morgan were a long way from food and drink and a place to sleep through the day. At worst they were the objects of a Line search that was dangerously near them. He had hoped for more from Morgan's wish than this. He himself wasn't sure exactly what, but Rigan would have known, and she'd have done it, too.

Morgan was scowling at him. "We've made the windsled go on without us, which was exactly what we were hoping to do. What's with you, anyway?"

"Two of the three wishes are used up," he muttered, "and we're a gods-rotting long way from Gorseth Arberth."

"You're lucky I didn't use the wish to make water from iron! That craziness you were dishing out about how magical we were —"

"We could have been Third Magic, for all they knew."

"But we weren't."

"Obviously," he almost snarled.

"I did my best, Arddu. If that isn't good enough —"

"And how do you know that horseshoe couldn't have taken us to Gorseth Arberth?"

"I *don't* know," she snapped. "I just had a feeling about the horseshoe, that's all. Just a feeling. Did you want me to waste a wish on something the horseshoe might not be able to do?"

He remained stubbornly silent. Why couldn't she be more like Rigan? With Rigan, he always knew where he was. He remembered the way Morgan had fed and watered those animals on the sled last night. She might almost have *been* Rigan then. Why couldn't she stay like that instead of —

He caught himself up, hard. Morgan wasn't Rigan. Morgan could never be Rigan.

"All right," he said, hugging his cloak to him like a shield. "You did your best, and we're here, and our legs are still working. So let's hurry up and use them."

"Which way?"

Arddu looked after the windsled, now a blazing dot on the horizon. "West, where else?"

"Will there be any water, do you think?" Morgan asked.

So already she was thirsty. He pulled his cloak even tighter, the unreasoning anger rising again. "The River Ffraw dips south between Awarnach and the sea," he said coldly. "We'll meet it sooner or later. Then we'll follow it to the ocean."

"And then? There was a ship, you said. We'll have to get in touch with it."

"You don't get in touch with *Kynthelig*," Arddu said. "You just go to Cwm Cawlwyd, and sometimes the ship is there."

"But how —?"

"Morgan, if we don't find somewhere to hide by dawn, we won't have to worry about the *Kynthelig* or anything else. If you're coming with me, come. And for the gods' sake, no more questions!"

She had no room for pride. She had no one but him in all Nwm. Head down, tears burning behind her eyelids, she picked her way through the stones of Eifionydd, following him.

ELEVEN

They will not make their cauldrons
That will boil without fire.
— Book of Taliessin VII
(Hostile Confederacy)

T HE moon was bright and unclouded, but in the dark, on
the rugged and broken plain that Eifionydd had become,
even Arddu would have been happy with more light. Morgan
felt worse than blind, dizzied by the rapid movement of the
moon. She leaped over potholes that weren't there and bumped
into rocks she'd just seen, all the while maintaining the grim
silence that was all Arddu seemed to want from her.

He knew she couldn't see, she told herself resentfully. Why
didn't he help her, or at least warn her of the worst parts? It
wasn't her fault she wasn't his marvelous Rigan!

The night wore on. Arddu remained silent, stopping only
to consult the stars. Now and then Morgan thought her vision
was getting better, and for minutes on end she would actually
walk without stumbling. But then, unaccountably, it would
worsen again, and she would catch her foot in a small burrow,
or blunder into the prickly spines of an unexpected bush.
"Are there snakes out here?" she asked once, imagining she
had heard a slither. Arddu only shrugged, but she noticed
that after that he trod a little more heavily. She imitated him
exaggeratedly until tiredness and hunger overrode everything
else. And still they plodded on.

Before dawn the lumpy plain began to descend, hills rising
on one side only to fall twice as far on the other, stone giving
way to grass, even here and there a struggling tree. The sky
was lightening to gray when in the distance they saw the river.

It lay like a furrow of smoke in the valley ahead, looping through lands whose ownership was divided between Line and Circle.

"It's still far," Arddu said, dismayed. He sent a swift, searching glance into the sky. There were no birds, not yet. "We'd better keep going," he muttered.

They hurried on. The sun rose quickly, once it began. In the distance, where a copse of trees grew beside a bend in the river, a great black flock of birds suddenly rose up, silent and purposeful. Morgan looked worriedly at Arddu, not quite daring to ask. He saw her look and shrugged.

"They're ravens," he told her. "They keep to their own business. Nothing to do with us."

"Are you sure?" If the Line could use hawks, why not ravens?

"The Line controls the birds of prey," Arddu said, "and the Circle the forest and water birds. But the ravens belong to nobody. Their only business is carrion."

The birds circled once, then suddenly flew off, straight as an arrow into the northeast. He frowned. "Something big must have died, for them all to go off at once like that."

He stood motionless, watching. The flock grew smaller and smaller, and then disappeared.

"How do they know something died, if it's that far away?" Morgan asked.

"They know."

"Awarnach is that way," Morgan asked uneasily, "isn't it?"

He didn't answer, and after a moment, they went on.

★

They reached the River Ffraw around the middle of the morning. Clouds had come shortly after dawn, hiding both sun and moon. There had been no time for daylight to steam off the dew, and water lay everywhere in little puddles. Even the air seemed gentle, the breeze not even related to the wild wind that had sucked the windsled through the desert. It sighed across the green tops of the reeds and puffed out the cobwebs netted between the cow parsnips. To Morgan, everything was beautiful. Her parched eyes drank it in, her nose sniffing up the green smell while the tension — and, strangely, her strength — drained out of her.

"We're sure to find somewhere to hide by the river," Arddu said over his shoulder. There was relief in his voice. "Hungry?"

She wasn't, not anymore. She shook her head, and her hood fell back. Her hair glittered almost silver in the daylight. "Cover your head," he ordered. She obeyed, blinking at him. "Morgan?" he asked. "Are you all right?"

"Fine." She smiled. "It's pretty here, isn't it?"

He took her arm and moved her toward the tall reeds by the river. She was limping. "You're hurt," he muttered, shame-faced.

"Queen Anne's Lace," she said dreamily, pointing to a brake of cow parsnips growing on the riverbank. "But so big!"

He had to urge her forward. The drier soil was covered with nettles, tall as a man. He touched one, then jerked his hand back, a red patch burning where the nettle had stung him. He turned and headed for more marshy soil. Here the giant leaves of the cow parsnip would hide them from hunting birds. The reeds were everywhere, their tall green stems sudsy with frogs' eggs. Arddu cleared a spot. Then he wrapped Morgan's cloak twice around her, and half pushed her into a prone position.

"All right?" he asked, looking a little anxiously at her white face.

"Just tired," she muttered.

He gave her a drink, then had one himself. "I'll get us some food later, when it's safe," he promised. She said nothing. He lay down beside her. Looking up, he could see only wisps of the sky through the deeply lobed leaves. Slowly the quiet sounds of the river took over: the *cree-creek, cree-creek* of insects, the lap and splash of water on stone, the rustle of the wind in the reeds. After a while their eyelids drifted shut.

★

Plop! Splash!

Morgan jolted awake. A frog, that was all, jumping off its lily pad into the river. She blinked up at the patches of gray sky visible through the leaves. The cow parsnips were pale outlines, almost colorless. Was it getting dark? Was that why she couldn't see? She tried to rub her eyes, but her arms felt too heavy to lift. Her head hurt, a knife stabbing into each temple.

"Arddu?" she croaked.

Her cloak was soaked through from the wet ground. With immense difficulty she turned her head to the place Arddu had slept. He wasn't there.

Somehow she got to her knees. She parted the reeds, peering this way and that into the twilight. Where was Arddu? At last she saw him, crouching and walking through the reeds, making his way from the riverbank toward her. He saw her looking and grinned, waving something in his hand. "Food," he said, when he was near enough. "I told you I'd get some."

It was a fish, dead and squishy and white. She thought she would vomit.

"Oh, no," he said softly, looking at her face. He laid his palm on her forehead. Then he struggled out of his cloak and wrapped her in it. "Lie down," he said.

"But we . . . we have to go . . ."

"You're sick," he said flatly. "We're not going anywhere."

★

Morgan slept, little beads of sweat on her forehead, her face so white that even the dark of a cloudy night could not hide her. Arddu came and went, making her his center, searching for someplace drier and safer to take her, for herbs to control the sickness, for food she might be able to stomach. He had found meadowsweet, which would reduce her fever and take away the pain. It was still steeping in his water pouch. But food was another matter. She would not eat the fish he had brought her, though it would restore her strength. There were plenty of frogs, too, but he shook his head. Clearly she would not eat anything raw.

Imagine depending on fire for food! If she had been well, he'd have simply let her get hungry enough to eat anything. But she wasn't well, and she wasn't hungry, and she had to eat or she would die. Which meant, he thought grimly, that he was going to have to learn to cook. And that meant fire —

obtaining it, carrying it, using it. Raised on Gorseth Arberth, and seeking fire!

It didn't cross his mind to abandon Morgan. It would have been like abandoning Rigan. Besides, with Morgan he had a reason to exist, something to do besides simply surviving. He would take her to Gorseth Arberth, and he would ask the Circle to send her home, and after that it wouldn't matter what he did.

He admitted it to himself, finally and completely, there in the quiet night on the edge of the river, a league from where she lay. He would be lonely without Morgan. Morgan was alien, but in many ways, so was he. Two misfits, he thought; but it was better than being one alone.

He walked on, looking for a cottage of the Line, a farmstead, any place that might have fire. As the night passed, he followed the river into the northeast, risking the lands near Awarnach, though the ravens had frightened him, heading that way. It was long after midnight when he found what he was looking for. It was a small dwelling set some distance back from the river, with empty fields where in the day cows would graze. The house was made of stone, so that Arddu wondered for a moment if perhaps the inhabitants had Circle loyalty after all. But when he went around to the other side, he saw on the wide lintel over the doorway a burning iron firepot.

With a sharp flint he ripped off a piece of cloth from the bottom of his tunic and wrapped his hand in it. Then he made his way slowly and nervously toward the doorway. Inside the house a dog gave a single loud bark. Arddu stopped dead. He was downwind of the house. It had to be noise, not scent, that had roused the animal.

Heart thudding, he waited, resisting the impulse to run. The dog was silent. Finally, he screwed up his courage and advanced again. The dog remained quiet. At last he was at the doorway, stretching as high as he could, grasping the iron handle of the firepot.

Almost in slow motion, he brought it down. It was hot, he could feel it even through the cloth, but it did not feel terrible to him. In a way its heat was even comforting. He would have to feed it, he thought, looking down at the glowing coals. He found a dead twig and dropped it into the pot, watching with interest as it flared up. Then he realized what he was doing and shivered.

He made his way back to the riverbank, then headed southwest, following the river toward Morgan. The Ffraw was the longest river in Nwm, not as wide or as fast as the Annan in the south, but colder than any other river, colder even than the ocean in winter. It had its roots in the north in the Mountains of the Moon, away past Awarnach and Tren in lands where no one went. Tonight the river was dull under the clouds, and its cold breath made him shiver.

He hurried along the bank with the firepot in his hands, shouldering his way through bushes that were already as lush as summer. He had left Morgan alone for a long time. What would she do if she woke up, delirious with fever, and he was not there? The thought made him want to run, but he controlled the impulse. It would do Morgan no good at all if he jounced all the coals out of the firepot before he had cooked her even one fish.

How long would they have to keep hidden before she would be well enough to move? Would she ever get well at all, lying on cold wet ground with that fever? But there was no point thinking of moving her to another hiding place. She couldn't walk, and though she was thin, she was too big for him to carry very far. He thought of stealing a horse, but from the looks of the steadings he had seen, the people here were poor, raising cattle for the Line or farming just to keep themselves alive. They would have no horses.

But they would fish. Line servients would do it from the bank, casting their rods and hating every moment. But Circle servients would use nets and boats, the Pwmpai's round coracles made of river reeds and withes.

Boats, Arddu thought.

In a boat, even a sick person could travel and still rest.

He made himself think it through. Two brown-cloaked fisherfolk in a coracle on the river. It would be a common enough sight, surely. He and Morgan might make it the whole way to Cwm Cawlwyd without catching the Line's attention. And if they didn't get that far, well, running water would stop most Second Magics.

But there were no boats on this side of the river. His eyes swept the opposite bank. There were no farmsteads in sight. He couldn't risk backtracking toward Awarnach with dawn so near. He would just have to continue on his way, and hope he'd be lucky.

The sky was paling when across the river he finally saw a steading downstream from him. It was beside a spit of land that jutted out into the water, half hiding what might be a wooden dock. The house was dug into the ground so that only the outline of its roof could be seen. Definitely not a Line dwelling, Arddu decided, looking at the conical shape.

Which meant there must be a boat. He closed his eyes, willing it to be so. Then he put down the firepot and stripped off his tunic.

Gods, but it was cold! He didn't dare hesitate. Taking a deep breath, he stepped onto a fallen tree overhanging the river, and dropped in.

He had never felt such cold. It slashed at him, invading every part of him at once. He came up for air gasping and wheezing, the current carrying him downriver from the tree. He would never make it, gods, oh gods! Desperately he began to swim, churning through the water with all his strength. The northern bank seemed leagues away. His arms cleaved through the current, powerful with fear.

The dock caught him. His arm hit it, and he hung on, too tired to haul himself out. But he had to, or he would freeze. Somehow he managed it. His bare feet padded down the wooden dock. He was shuddering with cold and exhaustion, but day was breaking, and he couldn't let himself rest. In the lee of the wind behind the dock, he found what he was looking for. It was a coracle with room for two adults and their gear. There was even a paddle in it. And there was a blanket. He got in. With fingers that fumbled and trembled and would hardly obey him, he wrapped the blanket around himself. Then, for one short moment, he let himself rest.

When the shuddering was less, he cast off. Taking the paddle, he worked his way out into the faster water. It had been a long time since he'd handled a coracle. He'd forgotten how obstinate they could be.

As he experimented with different strokes and felt his old skills return, a sudden joy overcame him. He was alive. He had a boat. He was even getting warm. And Morgan would be safe. Happily, he paddled for the opposite bank. He had no difficulty knowing where to aim. Like an idiot, he had left the firepot glowing, right out in plain view. He was too exhilarated to care.

He pulled up to the bank and dressed. Since he had left Morgan his cloak, he tore a strip off his tunic to hide his hair. Another scrap went to protect the bottom of the coracle from the firepot's heat. At this rate, he thought, if he ever did get to Gorseth Arberth, he would be stark naked.

The place where he had left Morgan was at least two leagues downriver, but he wasn't worried about finding it. He had marked the place by a pair of crossed saplings. He was a league on his way when a hawk passed overhead. He saw it, but made no attempt to hide. Dully and carefully he paddled on, acting the part of an ordinary fisherman out for his morning's catch.

Just think of your paddling, Arddu told himself. Pretend it isn't there.

Suddenly and wildly, the hawk screamed. Arddu jerked upright, shocked out of the role he was playing. But it didn't matter. The hawk was already gone, flapping madly into the northeast, toward Awarnach and the Line. What had he done? Arddu asked himself blankly. How had he given himself away?

And then he looked down and saw what the hawk had seen — a firepot of the Line in a coracle of the Circle; and he knew.

The Moon was full, high in the cloudless sky, and very bright: the kind of night the Morrigan had not seen in a long time. In her glass boat, Magic-made and strong as teardrops, she poled slowly along the sea coast, peering into the foamy waves. Arthur was sleeping, his small body half lost in the rushes at the bottom of the boat, his head pillowed on a bag of broom blossoms. He was ten now, a secretive, fine-boned child, smaller and older than his years, and full of opposing wisdoms. The M'rlendd trained him by day, and there was nothing the Morrigan could do about it; but the nights were hers, and all the loving. He was not yet hers, not completely, but he was even less the M'rlendd's. Until now the Morrigan had had to be satisfied with that.

They were a long way from home — if any place on this dim, poor world could be called that. Here there was only this barren coast and its iron-roofed hut, the M'rlendd with his ambitions and his suspicions, and Arthur. She made do, using infusions of broom blossoms instead of the rivers of Gorseth Arberth to give her visions, managing with flint in place of jade, with rushes from the River Cml instead of white mares' tails, with dandelion puffs where once she had used webs of the stonespider. And all done secretly, by the glimmer of Earth's pale moon: journeys taken while the M'rlendd slept; magics worked under the open sky in the dead of night; her shield sloughed off like skin when the sun set and put on again

111

*when it rose; and all the while doing the M'rlendd's bidding,
whatever he asked, whatever it cost.*

*She had been forced to dwell under an iron roof, forced to
eat meat, forced to use fire herself. She was female and anath-
ema to Second Magic, but lately he had been making her fetch
and carry for him while he worked, as if to emphasize his
invulnerability, or her servility. There were other things, too,
worse things. She tried to turn them all to her own advantage,
but what she gained in knowledge she lost in magic, and she
knew she was weaker. Sometimes, when the sun was hot and
rain scarce, when the M'rlendd's eyes lusted at her across his
smoky cave, she found herself wondering how much of her
own magic remained. And then she would call forth the glass
boat and spend another desperate night searching for the red
egg. It was how she survived.*

*Tonight she had gone far, farther than ever before. There
was something about this night, this moon. Tonight her hope
was strong. She seemed to know where she was going, even
what to look for. Ten years, she thought. Gods, would this
be the night? Suddenly her pole stilled. Her eyes narrowed,
staring into the moonlit sea.*

"Arthur!" she called, soft and strong. "Arthur, look!"

*He sat up, drowsily eager. "Did you find it, Morgan? Is it
really red?"*

*"See for yourself." Eyes triumphant, she pointed at the red
egg, solitary offspring of the giant sea serpent, laid in the
shallows only once in ten years. She had been searching for
it since Arthur's birth, and now she had found it: her chance
at the M'rlendd, her only chance, maybe, for his ultimate
control. Second Magic serpent coiled within First Magic egg
— keep it there, do not let it hatch, and by the Mother, she
had him!*

*"Can I get it for you?" Arthur asked, scrambling forward
in the boat.*

*She ignored him, sliding out of the boat, setting it gently
rocking. Both hands reached into the silver foam. Her face
was alight. Arthur said nothing, just helped her back into the*

boat with his eyes averted. She wrapped the precious egg in her cloak, and said, "You might have broken it."

He turned away. Shrugging, she picked up the paddle. She had the egg. Nothing else mattered, not even Arthur.

TWELVE

The White Town in the bosom of the wood!
There has ever been of its lustyhood,
On the surface of the grass, the blood!
— Red Book of Hergest XVI

PADDLING furiously toward the place where he had left
Morgan, Arddu tried to calculate the odds. How soon
could the Line organize a force to send downriver from Awar-
nach? Almost certainly it would be no later than midmorning.
That gods-rotting firepot! How could he have been so stupid?
He dug the paddle in so deeply he made the coracle spin.

The Red Cloaks wouldn't come in riverboats; no one con-
nected with the Line ever used them. And windsleds were
useless without roads. That left horses. Grimly Arddu con-
sidered it. Horses were fast enough to catch up to this little
coracle, given enough time. And it was a long, long way to
the ocean.

Should he abandon the coracle now that the Line knew
about it? But Morgan was too sick to find a new hiding place
on foot, and the Line would be turning its entire strength to
searching the river area. And Arddu didn't want to leave the
river. Its running water would protect him and Morgan from
Second Magic. Besides, in its meandering way the river was
heading in exactly the right direction. It emptied into the
ocean at Cwm Cawlwyd, which was the only place the Dreamer's ship *Kynthelig* received passengers for the island. He and
Morgan had to get there if they hoped ever to reach Gorseth
Arberth.

A stupid hope, he thought, for one already banished.

But at least if he and Morgan could get to Cwm Cawlwyd, there would be no more danger from the Line. Those of Line allegiance rarely went into the Pwmpai, and never in history had they penetrated as far as Cwm Cawlwyd.

The current was with him. Sooner than he'd hoped he saw the pair of bent saplings that marked where he had left Morgan. He pulled up and moored the coracle to one of the saplings. Scrambling out, he hurried to get Morgan. She was still sleeping under the cow parsnip, huddled into their two cloaks. Her face was as defenseless and trusting as if she had the whole Circle to protect her, instead of one magicless boy.

He roused her more roughly than he'd intended. Her eyes fluttered, the trusting look disappearing. "Drink this," he ordered, putting the water pouch to her mouth.

She swallowed the meadowsweet infusion thirstily, her second dose. He touched her forehead. Yes, the fever was lower. Food was what she needed now. He left her, hastily gathering some twigs and dried reeds. He dumped them into the bottom of the coracle, then added a few to the firepot's coals. Little blue flames licked up while he threaded two of yesterday's trout on a branch, then he hooked it over the top of the pot. Leaving the fish to toast, he went back for Morgan.

She was sitting quietly, her eyes half closed and vague. He began to lift her. Weakly she shook him off. "I can do it myself," she said resentfully.

"Do it, then." He was impatient, knowing how quickly time was passing.

"You never notice when I do things." Dismayed, Arddu saw that she wasn't speaking to him at all.

"Morgan —" he began.

"You're too busy to notice. I don't care. Mom and I don't care. We don't need you." Her eyes closed. "I told him. Mom? Are you glad? Mom?"

He shook her. "Wake up. Morgan, wake up!"

She blinked at him. "Arddu," she said, as if discovering who it was. Her eyes were focused. "Is it time to go?"

"Can you walk?" he asked. "It's not far."

She got to her feet. Arddu was careful not to help her. She was much less white, and managed the short distance to the coracle without difficulty. When she got in, she didn't say a word about the boat. Briefly Arddu resented her taking it for granted. Then he shrugged. Rigan would have been just the same.

Morgan curled herself around the firepot in the bottom of the coracle and immediately fell asleep. The sun was already much higher, but Arddu didn't leave at once. He wasn't hungry, but knew he ought to be. He had had nothing to eat since yesterday, and he was going to need all his strength today. He unwrapped one of the trout he had caught the day before. After three bites his hunger returned. He devoured two more of the fish, had a drink from the river, then untied the mooring rope and picked up his paddle.

Morgan slept. On the makeshift skewer over the coals her two trout sizzled cheerfully. As the day passed, the sizzling stopped. They must be cooked by now, Arddu thought. But he didn't remove them from the fire. He had been paddling so long he wasn't sure his hands could do anything else.

She hadn't even noticed that the fish were there.

★

Morgan awoke. The pain behind her eyes was gone. She felt like an oyster shell, all pearly and light with the sun shining through. Empty, clean, fresh as the sea. For a moment she lay without moving, too peaceful even to open her eyes.

Slowly she became aware of a rocking under her body, and the swish and trickle of water under a keel. She was in a boat. A real boat, not a windsled. And there was something warm nearby, something cooking, a wonderful smell of real food. Her stomach growled. She opened her eyes and saw Arddu.

"Hi," she said, smiling.

He didn't answer. He was paddling grimly, his face gray with fatigue.

"What's the matter?" she asked nervously.

He jerked his head upward. The evening sky was pierced with flying shapes: hawks, perhaps thirty or more. They stayed together, hanging like a storm cloud over the boat. Fear caught at Morgan. Weren't hawks solitary birds?

She sat up. Upstream from the coracle, more than a mile away, she guessed, were people. They were on horseback, a rust-brown mass of riders, perhaps fifty or sixty of them. "Red Cloaks!" she whispered.

"More than just Red Cloaks," Arddu said. "Look at the speed they're making. There are Linesmen with them."

The hawks overhead screamed. Morgan's nails cut into her palms. "Are we going to get away?"

"I don't know. We're close to Cwm Cawlwyd, but I never thought they'd come even this far." And in a whisper, not meant for her to hear, "Gods, but I'm tired."

She couldn't help. She'd never be able to paddle a boat like this. Desperately she looked around the coracle, for the first time noticing the fish over the firepot. "How long have you been paddling like this? Have you eaten? Are you hungry?"

He shrugged, and she reached for the trout hanging over the firepot. "Not those," he said, "they're for you. Mine are in those leaves."

She didn't know what to say. He had cooked her a meal. Arddu, who hated fire. And the coracle, too; and the long miles behind them. What else had he done while she lay sleeping?

Without a word she turned her head away, scrabbling in the leaves for one of the raw fish Arddu had caught. Once she would have been too disgusted even to touch it, but she found a sharp flint and hurriedly cut off a bite-sized piece of flesh, ignoring the juice that ran out onto her fingers. Then she fed it to him so that he wouldn't have to take his hands off the paddle. While he chewed, she made herself take the cooked fish off the firepot. Her stomach was acid with fear, and the dried-out, singed fish tasted like sawdust. But she ate it all, every bite. Arddu had done this for her. The least she could do was show she appreciated it.

The horsemen were gaining on them. Morgan could see them as individuals now, not just a mass of color. Arddu was looking over his shoulder more often, too, a jerky movement, tight with exhaustion.

"How far is Cwm Cawlwyd?" she whispered, not wanting to distract him, but desperate to know.

"Just around the next bend," he said. "They've got to stop soon. They've got to!"

"I could use the horseshoe," she said, pulling it out of her pocket. "There's still one wish left."

"The moon's behind a cloud. It might not work without it."

"If they're going to catch us anyway —"

He looked over his shoulder. The horsemen were falling back! He almost cheered. Then he realized why they had stopped. It wasn't because they were too afraid of the Circle to go on. It was because they were stringing longbows.

"They're going to shoot!" he shouted, grabbing Morgan's arm and pulling her flat.

"My horseshoe," she panted, scrabbling for it and getting in the paddle's way. "I dropped —"

The coracle was spinning. "Get back! I've got to paddle!"

Desperately, Arddu straightened the coracle again. The bend in the river was just ahead, a furlong, no more. Above their heads the hawks scattered, getting out of the way. The water swirled, caught by the river bend, fifty strokes away, forty . . . .

Twang! Twang! The sky was full of arrows. Feathers, hawks, arrows, points: and the coracle was pierced, again and again. Someone screamed. Then silence slammed down, complete except for the rushing water.

The coracle swept around the bend of the river. Two hawks followed the little boat, observing its motionless occupants, their white faces outlined by the glow from the firepot, their hair drifting and blending peacefully in the blood-stained, seeping river water. Just out of reach of the female's out-stretched hand was a semicircular piece of dark-green jade.

The coracle wallowed on. A furlong later it was passing the white sand banks of Cwm Cawlwyd. The hawks turned back. They had seen all that was needed. Tied up to the wharf was the ferryboat *Kynthelig*, and on her decks was the Dreamer.

★

In the cold of last night's moon, Llwch Llawynnog had dreamed: two passengers for the island, one the Morrigan, the other her brother. It surprised her that she would dream the male, who had already been Circle-banished, but it did not matter. Nor did it matter that the Morrigan must have returned to Nwm from Earth by non-Circle means. The dream demanded their passage to the island, and Llwch Llawynnog, Dreamer, could not disobey.

She frowned into the coracle as it lumbered by. Two healthy passengers: that was what she had dreamed, that was what she must deliver. She looked around her, at the white and empty beaches of Cwm Cawlwyd, at the hawks disappearing into the east, at the sun falling westward. Everything was exactly as she had dreamed it, everything except that her two passengers were dying.

Such a thing had never happened, the dream showing something falsely. Either the dream was wrong about the circumstances, or the circumstances must be changed to make the dream true.

A dream that must be aided, she thought. Her stomach turned, sick with dread.

She leaned out, catching the coracle with the boat hook, then fixing it so that the little boat was nestled into the *Kynthelig's* side. As she began to turn away, her eyes caught sight of something green at the bottom of the coracle. With her net she scooped it out of the water. It gleamed in her palm with a deep, ancient light: jade, Circle jade, a Made Magic halved. *It has been used*, she thought. And then, *I would know this thing, were it not so old*. And finally, *I do know this thing, and it should not be old*.

Llwch Llawynnog's pale, cold gaze went slowly and disbelievingly over the female lying so still in the coracle's deepening waters. A breath of a dream came to her and was gone, leaving only the scent of terror. Shuddering, Llwch Llawynnog wished she could just untie the coracle and let the sea swallow it. But wishes were meaningless. Only the dream mattered. And this dream insisted that this female and this male be brought alive to the island.

And so, with the shuffling, hunched steps of an old, old woman, Llwch Llawynnog went to make her preparations for healing.

★

The room was the color of shadow, pale, formless, empty of furnishings. Morgan became aware of it slowly, coming out of sleep like a diver surfacing. It was the smell that caught at her first, a scent like a forest, tangy with pine and violet and fresh as new leaves. She sniffed it in, reveling in the spongy feel of the floor under her. It absorbed her weight like peat moss in a bog. Too comfortable to move, she looked up at the ceiling. A pale light sifted through it, giving it the translucence of pearl. It had a depth that made it like sky. It did not seem man-made.

Of course it was not. The certainty was deeper than thought within her. No man had made this ceiling, or indeed any part of this room. Beside her on the floor, a boy stirred. She frowned, looking at him. What was a male doing in a place like this?

"Rigan," he whispered, opening his eyes and smiling at her hopefully. She only stared, and his smile faded. "Morgan," he muttered, "I forgot."

Morgan. She thought about this. Yes, she was Morgan. Memories returned, images flashing. A boat, a firepot; Celtic poetry in her father's voice; raw fish, hawks, horses, longbows . . . . And then iron, the pain of iron. A shudder went over her. She moaned, her hand clenching her arm.

He pried her hand away. Under it, her jacket sleeve was ripped. His fingers peeled back the torn cloth. "I thought so. You're fine, Morgan." He rubbed his own shoulder, adding wonderingly, "I am, too."

She blinked at him. "Arddu?" Then she looked down at the patch of unmarked skin on her arm. "But I was hit! The arrow was right here. It went through my arm and into my chest. Arddu, it happened!"

"We're on Gorseth Arberth," Arddu said. "Here there are lots of healers."

"But how did we get here?"

"The *Kynthelig*. It's the only way. The Dreamer must have been at Cwm Cawlwyd when we —"

He broke off. The room had been brightening as they spoke, the porous ceiling letting in more and more of the silvery light until even the dust hung in the air like bits of glitter. In the new illumination he noticed something for the first time. "They've taken away your cloak."

She stared down at herself. Her pink jacket and blue jeans looked wrong. It was this room, she told herself. Everything must look wrong in this glittering, icy room.

"How do we get out of here?" She hugged her arms to her chest.

"There's no door."

"We got in here somehow." She got up and paced rapidly, back and forth, up and down, all around the shapeless silvery room. There were no corners. There were no edges. There was only the silver dust, Arddu, and herself.

"We won't get out," he said. "Not until the Circle wants us to."

"At least they healed us. They wouldn't have done that if they had hated us. Maybe — oh, God, Arddu, do you think maybe they *will* send me home?"

"Do you still have your horseshoe?"

She thrust her hand into her pocket. Her face went white. "It's gone. But that doesn't mean — they still might —"

The chill of the room was in his skin, in his bones. The light was still growing. White, whiter, *could* it grow more white? He would have fallen except that there was no direction. Down was meaningless; there was no foundation. Everything was gone, nothing could be held onto. There was nothing in all the world but white.

None of those other times the Circle had questioned him had begun like this. For a moment he wondered what was happening. But then the ring of First Magic began circling in his mind, a blinding vice turning and turning, and it was the old nightmare all over again. Who are you? What are you? What are you hiding from us? Nothing was changed, and he had nothing to give them, nothing but the screaming of his lobed brain.

Morgan could see everything more clearly than she ever had in her life. A world away she saw her mother, pale with resentment, and her father, intense and dazzling. She saw a woman, round-bellied and middle-aged but with Morgan's own face; and she saw a crying boy running, a red egg in his hands. She could hear, too. She could hear breathing in all the darkened rooms of the world. She could hear the screech of the nightjar. She could hear the heartbeats of moles. She raised her hands to her ears, but could not stop the sounds.

And then the voices began.

Moon and Sun, gold rims about horns, cold are the paths.

White of skin, like us, like him.

The Line has meddled. Beware! I see a tree, bare of leaves, roots stretching even to Uffern.

Morgan clutched her head. But the voices bombarded her. She couldn't escape them. Pain lanced through her. She retched, again and again.

How many fingers about the cauldron?

Change, change, all changes. Whose is the grave in the circular space?

Accursed the maiden: She has let loose the sea.

"I'm not!" Morgan cried. "I didn't! I don't know what you mean!"

Thou hast pretended to be what thou art not.

"It's not my fault I look like Rigan. Send me home. Please. I never wanted you to think I was a Sister. I never even wanted to be one!" Morgan wept.

Silence suddenly, icy as the room. Then one voice only: *We ask thee, maid. Be the circle white or red?*

Morgan opened her mouth, but no sound came out.

White or red?

Tears poured down her face. She scrubbed at them with her sleeve.

A third and final time. Think well, before you speak. Be the circle white or red?

"I don't know. I don't know!" It was a shriek. She covered her face with her hands.

It is answer enough.

The Circle was gone. The whole white world blinked out. There was no imprisoning room; there were no doorless walls. There was only night and the deep forest of Gorseth Arberth, the spongy feel of peat moss, the tang of violets. In the darkness, Morgan fell to her knees. She didn't speak, not even when Arddu knelt beside her, not even when his arms went around her. Bruised and silent, they clung together until the night faded. Arddu felt her tears on his cheek, and they were his tears, too, as much his as if they had been wept from his own eyes.

The Circle had made its decision, and there could be nothing more final. Morgan and Arddu were going to have to stay on Nwm as long as they lived.

And how long that was going to be, only the Circle could say.

THIRTEEN

The Sibyl foretells a tale that will come to pass.
— Black Book of Caermarthen, XVII

T HE day passed. They stayed on the beach near the forest.
The whole island must have known they were there, but
no one disturbed them. Arddu kept himself moving, sharp-
ening an old flint knife and mending a water pouch he had
found, then fishing with someone's torn and discarded net.
Morgan sat numbly by herself, and she ate the fish he gave
her without even noticing that it was raw.

She had lost her world. Dimly Arddu could see the enor-
mity of that. Maybe losing the only place in the universe you
belonged was worse than never having found one at all.

There had been no further interference from the Circle.
Arddu was sure he knew why. The Sisters were trying to
decide between killing the two of them directly or turning
them loose for the Line to take care of. Ordinarily the Circle
would not balk at a killing. But this time the Sisters might
decide that they could learn more of the Line's plans by letting
the two of them go. Whichever plan they decided upon, Arddu
knew he and Morgan would be dead very soon.

As dusk approached, even Arddu grew still. It had been a
long time since either of them had slept, and without meaning
to, they fell into an uneasy doze on the beach. Sunfall came
and went, and their sleep deepened. And very late in the
black-and-white night, Morgan awoke, and out on the moonlit
sea she saw a silver ship sailing.

★

Twice already the Circle had asked Llwch Llawynnog to dream.

But no matter what she did, the dream would not come. And without the dream, the *Kynthelig* could not sail. Another Sister had come to Llwch Llawynnog in her shipboard cabin, pressing on her the urgency of getting the false Morrigan and the A'Casta away from the island. Still the dream did not come. The sun fell from the sky, and Llwch Llawynnog brooded about change, about dreams that must be aided, and dreams that would not be bid. And now and then, like an old nightmare, she thought about the real Morrigan, a Sister to whom the Circle had lied.

A joint decision, it had seemed, the entire Circle having pretended that the reason Gwyar, Heledd, and Elphin had gone off-island was to end the west's trade with the windsleds. The Morrigan had believed the lie. She knew, as they all did, that First Magic was diminishing as Second Magic grew. She knew that starving the Line was a way to reverse that process. She knew it would mean war, and no guarantee of victory. She knew that at best the Line would be weakened, not destroyed.

But she didn't know about the sword.

It had been the Dreamer who had dreamed of the sword's existence and the power it had. Because of her dream, Gwyar and Elphin and Heledd had been sent north to find the Sword and bring it to the Circle. They did not dare tell the Morrigan. She was First Magic, but she had *that brother*. She shielded herself from her Sisters when she was with him. She must not be told about a weapon that could destroy the Line.

As Llwch Llawynnog had said, "If she is a true Sister, we will know it, because no Line forces will be sent to reinforce the windports. She will not have betrayed us. If she is treacherous, at least her misinformation will keep Line eyes away from the north. Either way we will discover finally what the Morrigan is. Our suspicion has weakened the Circle too long."

They had thus given the Morrigan a chance to betray them, allowing her to meet her brother before they banished him and before she left on her missioning. The Line had taken him, of course, but no Line forces had been sent to arm the windports. So the Morrigan had been a true Sister. A Circle

125

member had been lied to. The Circle, like the Morrigan's jade circlet, had been broken, perhaps irreparably.

Unless the sword could save them. But Gwyar and Elphin and Heledd had been gone now for three seasons, and in the last two not even a bird had seen them.

My responsibility, Llwch Llawynnog mourned, deep in her soul. And grieving, suddenly, the dream came to her.

The images struck, wild as lightning and equally uncontrollable. She saw Gwyar riding alone through the Pwmpai; she saw Cwm Cawlwyd violated; she saw Gwyar's white mare suddenly riderless. And on the mare's back, through white wrappings, she saw a glitter of silver and knew that it was the sword.

Three Sisters had gone to find it. They had succeeded, but at what cost! Elphin, gone; Heledd, too. And Gwyar . . .

Dry-eyed, the Dreamer dreamed still. An image: her own white hand holding out the broken jade magic; the Line-summoned female taking it. Another: the girl and the A'Casta dropping over *Kynthelig*'s side into a rowboat. Oars splashing. Sand and silence. Cwm Cawlwyd. Hurry!

With a wrench the dream ended. Grim-faced, Llwch Llawynnog went out on deck, yanking at ropes, hauling up the anchor. The *Kynthelig*'s sails filled with wind, soft and sweet as a thousand journeys. It did not care, she thought. It obeyed the dream, and did not care. And for the first time ever, Llwch Llawynnog knew what it was to hate her ship.

★

Morgan sat up, shivering in the cold wind blowing in off the sea. Ever since they had taken away her cloak, she had been cold, but at first she had been too lost in despair to notice. Now she hugged her arms to her and tried to think of hot chocolate, of furnaces coming to life on a cold winter's morning, of bathtubs wreathed with steam. But these things were growing increasingly distant to her, like outlined pictures empty of texture and color. It frightened her that they seemed so dim, that she couldn't even really remember her mother's face. It frightened her even more how familiar the island was growing.

She was looking out to sea when *Kynthelig* came.

Arddu woke as she scrambled to her feet. "So they're going to let us go," he said.

He felt no joy that they were to be allowed to live a little longer. He felt no sorrow about leaving the island. Now he knew this was not his home. No place in all of Nwm was that.

The *Kynthelig* turned into the wind, dropping anchor. Sails came down silently. Out on the water Llwch Llawynnog climbed into a trailing dinghy. In silence they watched as she untied the boat, then picked up the oars and began to row toward them. There were almost no waves, and the boat left a wake like unrolling silk. Moon and stars glittered in the water dripping from her oars. Behind her, dark as a dream, the *Kynthelig* rode at anchor. When the dinghy was within wading distance of the shore, the old woman stopped rowing. Her back was to them, and she didn't turn around. She waited.

"We're being invited aboard," Arddu said.

They waded out. The old woman still said nothing. They climbed in, shuddering in their wet clothing, and even before they were properly seated, the dinghy was beginning its return journey. They reached the *Kynthelig* without another word spoken. On board, the woman turned away at once, setting sail and unlashing the tiller. The wind was light but icy as a breath from the moon. Taking Morgan's arm, Arddu headed for the solitary cabin. There would be no shivering in the bow for him, not this time.

Inside the cabin, Morgan and Arddu wrapped themselves in blankets. "Take the bed," Arddu said to her. "You might as well be comfortable."

She didn't argue. Neither expected to sleep, but they did, deep and dreamless, while the rest of the night slipped by. In the east, streaks of color announced the approach of dawn. Llwch Llawynnog steered for it, her eyes bitter as the night.

The sun rose. Morgan awoke with a blaze of gold in her eyes. Sunshine was streaming in from a porthole. She sat up, yawning. It seemed strange to wake up in a bed. She hadn't slept in one since . . .

Earth.

The familiar sickness turned in her stomach. She buried her face in the pillow. She would never see Earth again. She would never see her mother or her father again.

Mom, I miss you, Mom! And a whisper, *Dad*.

"We're almost at Cwm Cawlwyd." Arddu was at the porthole, scanning the lonely beach ahead.

"Who cares?" Morgan said, her voice muffled.

"We should talk about what we're going to do."

"What's the point?" she said, looking up. "Wasn't it you who said that if the Circle wouldn't have us, the Line would?"

"And in the chasm wasn't it you who said you didn't want to just sit there and wait for them?"

"That was before."

"We've got to at least work out our direction," he said stubbornly.

Her eyes were brilliant. "Right. Eenie, meenie, minie, mo. East, west, south, north. We go north. Direction worked out."

He stared at her. North? She was mad! No one lived in the north; no one who wanted to stay alive even went there. It was a condemned land, lost to humanity, a killer. The terrible names came to him: Redynvre, the endless maze; the Mountains of the Moon; Lyn y Van Vach, Lake of the Severing; and most perilous of all, the Yspyddadon, the Glass Giant, ruling with fire in one hand and ice in the other.

They couldn't go there.

But it was the one direction the Line might not expect. And could even the north be worse than being caught by the Line?

He looked doubtfully at Morgan. She was staring down, slamming her fist into her palm again and again. For the first time in a long while he could hear her thoughts quite plainly. He shook his head, ashamed but defiant. He had lost a lot, too, he told himself. She wasn't the only one who had a right to be unhappy.

The *Kynthelig* shivered, then again, and a third time. Anchor chains rattled. "We're here," Arddu said. "Morgan?"

She looked at him, then sighed and got to her feet. When the cabin door opened they were standing together, their backs to the wall, waiting. But Llwch Llawynnog didn't come in. She merely stood in the doorway. In the bright light her face was dark, a map of cracks and crevices where only the pale eyes were alive.

Arddu couldn't help it; he had to ask. "Is the Line near?"

The Dreamer's lips thinned, but she said nothing. Suddenly she thrust out her hand. It was closed tight, a blue-knuckled fist held palm upward. They watched it as if mesmerized, unable to move. Slowly and unwillingly, her fingers opened. And in her white palm they saw a small piece of jade.

"My horseshoe!" Morgan cried, starting forward.

"It is not yours," Llwch Llawynnog said, her first words, harsh and venomous. "It is Circle Magic, and you are no true Sister."

"Then why are you giving it back to me?"

"Dreams do not deal in right and wrong. You have a destiny. We all have a destiny." The old woman's hand shook, the dark green jade gleaming.

Convulsively Morgan reached for it. As her fingers closed around the little horseshoe she felt the old woman's palm, dry and cool and gentle-rough. A female hand, she thought, a mother's hand. A sudden memory came to her, vivid and alive, of her own mother working cream into her hands, rubbing, massaging, removing the roughness, the signs of her strength. It was a thought Morgan had never had before, and it filled her with sadness.

The moment the jade was in Morgan's grasp, Llwch Llawynnog jerked around, heading back out on deck. Only Arddu saw her face, and it made his heart thud.

He took Morgan's arm, hurrying her out. They were anchored a short way from shore. The sand dunes gleamed, rolling and empty and startlingly white against the blue of the sky. The sea was roughening, white water foaming against the shore. Back beyond the dunes tall grasses rippled, a wind movement, inhuman. Otherwise everything was still. There were not even any birds.

He didn't notice this at first, except to be grateful that there were no hawks. Then, suddenly, he knew. No sandpipers pecking in the shallows; no gulls swooping; no cranes; no cormorants. No Circle birds at all. And the *Kynthelig* anchored

129

offshore, not moored in the mouth of the river in the usual way. Fear rose metallic into his mouth.

So the Line was here.

Wild ideas came and went: to throw themselves on Llwch Llawynnog's mercy, to take over the *Kynthelig*, to sail her away where no one could ever find them. But none of it was any good. The *Kynthelig* sailed only where her mistress dreamed. Llwch Llawynnog had no desire to help them, and she was too strong in magic for them to force her.

"Get into the dinghy," Llwch Llawynnog said. "Now."

She was not looking at them. Her eyes were straining northward along the beach. Arddu followed her gaze, but saw only white sand and a distant cloud that looked like dust. "Why should we go?" he demanded belligerently. "If we're going to die anyway —"

But it was Morgan who answered him. "We have to do it," she said. "We have to be there."

He stared at her. What was she talking about? Her mind was open to him, but he shut it out, unable to face the certainty in it. How could she be so sure of something he didn't understand at all? "Make a wish," he ordered her roughly. "Use the horseshoe!"

"I can't," she said. The little dinghy was floating alongside, a rope ladder hanging into it. Without another word, Morgan began climbing down. Helplessly, Arddu followed her. They both looked up at the old woman, waiting for her to join them. But she was staring north, unmoving. Arddu looked, too. The dust-cloud had turned into a white horse galloping toward them, ridden by someone in a black-and-silver cloak.

"Go!" Llwch Llawynnog cried, high and cracked. "Mother take you, go!"

And Morgan took up the oars, and they went.

FOURTEEN

Like a boar didst thou lead to the mount,
There was treasure for him that was fond of it;
There was room;
And there was the blood of dark-brown hawks.
— Book of Aneurin I (The Gododin)

ELPHIN had died in the mountains. Heledd had died, too, in the Fire of Glass. Now there was only Gwyar. From Heledd's melting fingers Gwyar had received the sword, though by then she had known its peril, and had longed to refuse it. But two Sisters had died, and a Dreamer had dreamed the sword's value, and so Gwyar had taken it.

In the weeks that followed, she had discovered more about the sword. She grew thinner, forgetting to eat. Her silver eyes sank like stones into her face. She wrapped the sword in white linen, and would not touch it. She began to talk aloud to her mare, Cynfarch. "It wasn't the Fire that killed Heledd," she said one day, into the ringing northern silence. And then, later, "It will kill me, too, Cynfarch."

A sheath of stone, a tower of glass, a ring of boiling water, a plain of melted stone. Coming from all this, was it any wonder the sword possessed such magic?

Each day the sword grew stronger and more determined. It didn't want to be here. It wanted to be returned to its own place. Gwyar almost obeyed it a dozen or more times, reining in a reluctant Cynfarch, half turning in the saddle to look back to the north; then, somehow, refusing. "Such power, Cynfarch," Gwyar would whisper then. "Mother save us, such power!"

In Circle hands this sword would sever the Line a million times over, cutting it to pieces as small as the worms of the earth. Gwyar knew that. But she could only guess what wielding it would do to the Circle.

"We are going home, Cynfarch," Gwyar would say, time and again through that terrible northern journey. And the white mare would shake her head until sparks crackled off her mane and the only way to stop her was for Gwyar to lean forward and lay her cheek against Cynfarch's. That was when Gwyar would weep for the Circle, and for Nwm. She grew thinner still, drained by her tears.

When they passed into the northern Pwmpai she tried to rejoice, knowing herself once again in Circle territory. But she could not. Each hour brought the use of the sword closer. She tried not to think of this. They went west to the ocean, then southward, heading for Cwm Cawlwyd. Gwyar allowed her magic to sleep, knowing how much it needed recovery, but she herself could not rest. Cynfarch was tireless, riding alongside the same ocean that bathed Gorseth Arberth. While Gwyar sat slumped in the saddle, league after league went by. Suddenly Cynfarch lifted her head into the wind and whinnied. Jerked out of her reverie, Gwyar saw an unmistakable spit of land jutting into the ocean. "Cwm Cawlwyd!" she cried. Cynfarch whinnied again, then bounded forward.

Out to sea a white ship was making for Cwm Cawlwyd. A rush of delight swamped Gwyar's numbness. "The Dreamer is coming for us, Cynfarch!" she cried. The mare heard her excitement and increased her speed, stirring up sand in a white and glittering cloud.

Out on the water the *Kynthelig* dropped anchor, and two people climbed into the little dinghy alongside. Suddenly Gwyar pulled up and dismounted, holding Cynfarch still. Something was wrong. The *Kynthelig* never anchored this far offshore. Gwyar watched as the dinghy headed toward land. She recognized the two people in it: the Morrigan at the oars, but — wrong, all wrong — wearing no cloak; and her brother, the A'Casta, a passenger.

Gwyar's magic was awake now, and seeking. In her mind she sensed a searing and a stench of burning. The Line was in Cwm Cawlwyd! She tried to turn, but Second Magic held her. Cynfarch reared, neighing wildly. The reins slipped from Gwyar's hands.

The Line must not get the sword! Blackness gushed like blood through Gwyar's body. *Tired*, a tiny part of her wailed, *Mother, I'm so tired!* But she was a Sister, and this was Cwm Cawlwyd. How dare the Line come here! She jerked free from the Line's mental grasp and turned toward the dunes. Her eyes were darkening, the pupils devouring her silver irises and the whites of her eyes. Cynfarch reared and reared, trumpeting a challenge to the rolling sand hills. But Gwyar stood still, a statue with two jet-black jewels for eyes.

And then, as the two occupants of the little dinghy stumbled out onto the pier and began desperately to run down it toward the silent Sister, the Line attacked.

★

The Red Cloaks were on foot, the horses having been sent back to Awarnach at the beginning of the first interminable night. The reek of First Magic in Cwm Cawlwyd had ruined all control of the Line-trained beasts, and it had done little better for the men. The strangeness of the place had affected even Unwch, the Linesman who had volunteered to remain at Cwm Cawlwyd with Menw Line-End when the others had gone back to the town. Menw had taken it upon himself to avenge fully the murder of the Sdhe. He wanted to wait for a message from the Line's spy on Gorseth Arberth, verifying the Morrigan's death.

At dawn the falcon came. The message contained mixed tidings. The Morrigan had not died, but for some reason she was out of favor with her Sisters. She would be banished, and her brother with her. As soon as the Dreamer dreamed, the two would be returned to Cwm Cawlwyd.

And so Menw and Unwch waited, and their men, shifting and white-eyed, waited with them.

But no one had expected that Sister riding in from the north.

"Gods burn it, Line-End, there are three! You said there would be only the Dreamer and the Morrigan!"

Menw did not share Unwch's fury. He knew the girl they called the Morrigan had no magic. Nevertheless, overcoming two Sisters would be difficult, especially as the Dreamer had remained on water, where Second Magic could not touch her. As well, the unexpected Sister was out of range of their bows. He frowned.

"We two will deal with the Sister from the north," he announced brusquely. "Our Red Cloaks must take care of the Morrigan on their own."

"Without our help, they won't be able to kill her. She'll use the Spelled Death on them. They'll die like —"

"I have spoken," Menw said tightly.

Unwch allowed himself a single blazing look. Then he sent the command.

★

Swordsmen were rushing toward the pier. Terrified, Morgan pelted down it, following Arddu. She could hear the twang of bows, but so far there were no arrows. She reached the end of the pier only moments before the red force. Leaping onto the sand, she sprinted after Arddu, leading for that unknown Sister whose glittering black eyes were visible even this far down the beach. Shouts and the clash of metal intensified behind her.

I should have listened to Arddu, Morgan thought. I should have made a wish! But if she stopped running now she'd be dead before she could even get the horseshoe out of her pocket.

Her eyes throbbed in rhythm with the hammer in her heart. She could barely see. Arddu was just a brown and fuzzy outline pumping along beside her. The Sister herself was nothing but a black-and-silver patch; faceless, for all that Morgan could see. But there were things inside that Sister, things Morgan *could* see. It was like that dream she'd had on Earth when she had known everything Rigan was thinking about the pregnant woman with her. Now Morgan was seeing another Sister's thoughts and identifying with them as if they were her own: the hopeless longing for a homeland she would never again see; the hatred; the questions. Why me? Life and death and rot and afterlife, and then all to be done again, and for what? For what? Heledd had died. Elphin had died. She would die, too. What did one life matter?

As long as the Line did not win.

Running, Morgan stumbled. She gasped out Arddu's name. His strong hand closed over her wrist, hauling her up and dragging her along until her legs coordinated again. Her mind was wide open to him. He couldn't shut her out, he heard everything: the loneliness, the futility, the emptiness of moon-less skies, the longing for home. A boy was crying, and she was wiping up blood; a glass boat; a red egg.

The Line will not win, Arddu. Whatever happens, whatever I must do, the Line will not win.

With a cry, he dropped Morgan's hand. "Rigan?"

She was running on without him. Quaking with terror, Arddu sped after her. "Morgan!"

She was a Sister. She was all Sisters. "I'll help you!" she cried. "Gwyar! Sister! I'll help you!"

Through the fire of Second Magic, Gwyar heard. Shielding herself tiredly, she looked at the girl running toward her. Why was the Morrigan coming straight here? She should have circled around toward the sea, where with the Dreamer they might have tried Encircling the Linesmen. But something was weakening the Dreamer's magic: hopelessness, perhaps; a foreknowledge of the outcome of all this. Perhaps the Mor-rigan knew the Dreamer could not be relied upon for help. Perhaps she, too, guessed the outcome.

But at least the sword might be prevented from going to the Line. She could not do it, the Line was concentrating all its forces on her. But the Morrigan seemed relatively free. There was something she could do, something they all could do. The unnatural blackness in Gwyar's eyes broke up, letting in silver light like stars. The Morrigan was nearly there, run-ning to her with love and understanding in her face. *My Sister,* Gwyar thought. She forgot that the Morrigan didn't even know the sword existed. She forgot everything but necessity. "You'll save the sword, Morrigan?" Gwyar pleaded. "It's not for us, but it must not be for them, either!"

135

"I'm not —" Morgan began, reaching out a hand toward that white, beautiful face.

"Cynfarch will bear you. I am already dead. Ride!"

Arddu waited for no more. He grabbed the pommel of Cynfarch's saddle and swung himself up, dragging Morgan behind him. There was no time for anything else. Wheeling the great white horse about, he headed north up the beach. Pain attacked him, hot and deadly as fire. The mare screamed, and Morgan did, too. But they had been too far away when the Line had first seen what was happening, and Gwyar was still a force to be reckoned with. The white horse kept going, galloping up the dunes in a cloud of sand.

They were already a long way away. Arddu looked over his shoulder past Morgan's gray face and tight-closed eyes. Cwm Cawlwyd had been a white place, but now it was red, a lake of red surrounding the tiny, shimmering white island that was Gwyar. All at once that island disappeared, swallowed by the red. And from somewhere, gods knew where, the ravens began to circle.

She had been brave. Arddu gave her that tribute. He turned away, digging his heels into Cynfarch's flanks and setting his gaze sternly into the northeast, away from the ocean, away from Cwm Cawlwyd. A white bundle bumped into his knee, but he ignored it. He said nothing to Morgan, nor she to him. They crossed the first set of dunes, and the second. Not even a bird followed. There was nothing to look back for, nothing but sand and sky.

Behind them, out of sight on the water, the *Kynthelig* was setting sail. Trembling and sick, Llwch Llawynnog hauled on ropes and released the tiller, felt for the wind and found it. In her mind reeled the tidings she would have to relate to the Circle. Gwyar, dead, destroyed, not even a body remaining to go into the earth for rebirth. Gwyar's two Sisters gone, too, lost to the Circle forever. The A'Casta and the female heading north, the sword with them. Did they know what they had? And the Linesmen who would follow, more and more of them raging through the Pwmpai and farther, fighting the Circle wherever they met, aiming to be the first to reach the two with the sword. And they must not be first! They must not!

She fought for calm. She was Dreamer; she must be in control. But the dream had turned to nightmare, and she had not been able merely to watch it and not care.

The wind blew into her face, icy cold, stinking. Clouds blanketed both the moon and the sun. White-knuckled, Llwch Llawynnog sailed westward. Her final journey, she thought. There would be no one to replace her.

The age for dreaming was over.

PART III

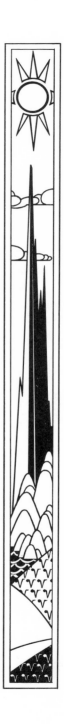

He had broken the egg.

There was a heath where stood a ring of stones, a place of powers the Morrigan understood. She had wept the first time she saw it, and never gone back. Now she sat there, alone under a mocking sun, realizing her disaster.

How could Arthur have done this thing?

The red egg smashed, the serpent inside escaped. The ten-year search wasted, useless as the four magic-weakening years of spells that had followed. The loss was deep. It cut the Morrigan like shards of bitter glass, blood-bringing and stinking of endings.

Not that the egg had ever fulfilled all her hopes. It had managed to contain part of what the M'rlendd was, but never all. Over the four years she had tried to spell the man into the egg, somehow the bits of him that the egg couldn't imprison grew. Adapting, always adapting. And as the Morrigan's magic strained to keep the M'rlendd small, it was she who grew less, and he who merely waited out the nights.

And not only waited.

She looked down at her belly, thick with child. It would be a boy. She knew this: knew, too, the color of its eyes.

Her long white fingers rubbed at her temples. What would her Sisters in the Circle have done differently? What would they do now? The long war of guile and spells over, and Earth unencircled. Arthur lost forever. And a child to account for, a boy-child. The son of a Linesman and a Sister!

The M'rlendd's fault. All of it, his. All.

The stone at her back felt hard and comfortless. In this place it was impossible not to acknowledge the truth. The M'rlendd was only partly to blame. The rest of the fault was her own. She had seen Arthur's face the night she had found the egg, his longing to touch the egg himself, but she had paid no attention, she had denied him. She had forgotten the lure of the magical to one who has no magic, the curiosity of the M'rlendd-trained. She had placed her trust in Arthur's love, forgetting that love is a First Magic, and that all Arthur's days were spent in Second.

The breaking point had come when Arthur had learned of the child the Morrigan bore. "You don't spend time with me as it is!" he had shouted. And then, unforgivably, he had told her to get rid of the baby, as his mother had him.

"I am no Ygerne," she had replied with dislike, "and my babe is no Arthur, to be abandoned."

From that moment he had spied on her, and he had found the egg where she had hidden it, and in his curiosity or jealousy or misery, he had destroyed it.

Error upon error. Her fault, as much as the M'rlendd's.

Arthur had found the broken circlet of jade, also. He could not destroy it, but he had taken one of the halves. That, too, was partly her fault, because she had let him see how much she valued it. Ever since the egg had proved itself imperfect, mending the circlet had become her obsession. Night after night she had left Arthur with the M'rlendd while she searched for different herbs or better spell-circles to try to mend it. And when Arthur had wakened, calling her, she had not been there.

She understood perfectly why he had done what he did with the jade. Take one of the pieces, and the whole could never be mended. Leave the other, and she would be continually reminded that something she desperately wanted was unattainable. It was an act of malice far in advance of his smashing the egg. That had put Arthur irrevocably on the side of the M'rlendd, but leaving her that solitary piece of jade had made him her enemy.

Twenty-nine years I have been on Earth! Mother, Sisters, gods, please, let me come home!

But she couldn't mind-seek a summoning, not with all these failures to carry back to Nwm with her. She must atone for the loss of Earth's Encirclement. She must keep her vow that the Line would not win this world. She must make the M'rlendd fail as she had failed!

She still had some magic left, and she still had half the jade, with all its unknown powers. She had never used it, because she had hoped to keep its magic intact for when it was mended. But now she would not hesitate.

No longer was this a war she hoped to win. It was atonement, that was all. Circle payment for a plan gone awry, and private payment for twenty-nine wasted years.

It was revenge. And she no longer cared what she had to give up to get it.

FIFTEEN

He who takes hold of a wolf's mane without a club
In his hand, must naturally have a brave disposition
Under his cloak.
— Book of Aneurin I
(The Gododin)

THEY rode for a long time. In the cold blue sky the tireless moon circled. There were no clouds, but Arddu and Morgan seemed always to be riding in shadow. It didn't matter what time of day it was; their own shadows always preceded them. "North," Arddu muttered once, an explanation or a curse, but Morgan was shivering into his back and didn't reply. He thought of offering her his cloak again, but knew it would do no good. She was as stubborn as Rigan, when she wanted to be.

They were halfway through the Pwmpai, heading due north, and the sand dunes of the coast were only a blur on the western horizon. The Pwmpai was a rich land, sprouting fields stretching east as far as the eye could see, nurtured by the waters of the Ffraw and the blessings of the Circle. Farms dotted the flatness of the landscape, marked by First Magic granaries. These were spherical structures thrust halfway into the ground. The farmers used them for storage at harvest, but as well the granaries had Circle purposes that servients could only guess at. Arddu kept Cynfarch as far away from them as he could.

It was well past noon, and they had been riding since dawn. Arddu shifted in the saddle, easing an ache. It had been a long, rough ride.

For the first time since they'd run along that beach toward Gwyar, he let himself read Morgan's thoughts. Mixed with

143

dim memories of her own people were vivid, hating ones of the M'rlendd. There was one new face, too, a thin-cheeked, eager boy; but no images of Rigan, none at all.

He thought this over, riding onward. "Do you remember those dreams you used to have on Earth?" he asked her, staring straight ahead. "About Rigan and the M'rlendd?" She didn't respond. "I was just wondering, well, if you ever dreamed about them here."

"I dream about a lot of things," she said into his shoulder. "Sometimes I think —"

"What?"

"Nothing." Then, suddenly, "I know too much, Arddu."

"About what?" he asked.

"Everything. Nothing. It doesn't matter."

He turned his eyes on her, while Cynfarch plodded on. Morgan was the first to look down. "I do dream about Rigan," she said finally. "And there's a boy, too. He's called Arthur."

There was something odd about the way she said the name 'Arthur.' "What are you trying to tell me?" he asked, frowning.

"Remember how you said that to Encircle Earth maybe all Rigan would have to do was influence just one really important person?" He nodded. "Well, there was a *King* Arthur on Earth who was as important as that. And King Arthur had a magician named Merlin —"

"The M'rlendd!"

"That's just what I was thinking. And King Arthur's sister was called . . . Morgan LeFay." Arddu jerked on the reins, but she didn't give him time to speak. " 'LeFay' means 'the fairy.' People called King Arthur's sister that because she was magical. And so is Rigan."

"So you think," Arddu said slowly, "that when Rigan went to Earth she became Morgan LeFay?"

"It makes sense," she said.

"There are histories about this Morgan LeFay?" he asked, suddenly eager.

"It's mostly about what she did for Arthur. He was a great man, Arddu. People on Earth still talk about him, even though he lived fifteen hundred years ago. He had a wonderful sword called Excalibur that he pulled out of a stone — though some

144

people say a hand rose from the lake and gave it to him. That sword was how he got to be king. And he had a lot of knights who fought evil, the Knights of the Round Table. It was one of King Arthur's knights who found the Holy Grail. But by then, everything was going wrong."

None of this interested him. "What about Rigan?"

"I'm getting to her. You see, the reason everything was going wrong for King Arthur was because of his nephew, Mordred." She coughed a little nervously.

"His nephew?" Arddu repeated uncomprehendingly.

"His sister's son." She cleared her throat. "Morgan LeFay's son, I mean. The legends all say that she was Mordred's mother. And since we've already figured out that Morgan LeFay was Rigan — ."

Arddu didn't know why he was so shocked. He'd been the first to say Morgan was descended from Rigan. For that to be possible, obviously Rigan would have had to have a child. But to know it was a son, even to know the boy's name! For a moment he couldn't say anything. He turned in the saddle, gave an unnecessary twitch to Cynfarch's mane, and straightened his cloak. Then, keeping his eyes forward, he asked as calmly as he could, "Who was . . . Mordred's . . . father?"

"I don't know."

"Did Mordred grow up to be a good man?"

"Mordred? He was *horrible*. He practised black magic and he hated his uncle, the king. He would probably have been Arthur's heir in the end, but that wasn't soon enough for Mordred. He tried to break up the Round Table, and finally there was a terrible battle where both Mordred and Arthur were killed. There is a legend, though, that someday Arthur will come back to life. Morgan LeFay saved his body by taking it to a magical place called Avalon."

"Rigan saved Arthur, and not her own son?"

"She loved Arthur," Morgan said. "He was worth loving. And he was her brother."

There was something large and hard in Arddu's throat. He cleared it away. "Mordred must have fathered a child before he died," he said, "or you wouldn't be here. Unless, maybe, Rigan had a second child on Earth?"

145

"I don't think so," Morgan said. "I wish she had. I'm not crazy about having someone like Mordred for an ancestor."

"What happened to her in the end?" He couldn't keep the longing out of his voice.

"I'm not sure," she said. "Merlin was finally defeated by a powerful sorceress — that might have been Rigan. Or she might have stayed with King Arthur in Avalon, wherever that is. The trouble is, it's all so long ago."

"Not to me, it isn't," Arddu said. And for the rest of the day he hardly spoke a word.

★

It was almost evening. The meal they had shared on the beach of Gorseth Arberth seemed much more distant than a day ago. But they kept riding, knowing that all too soon the Line would have its own horses and be after them. Arddu's stomach was aching with hunger when Morgan asked wistfully, "Do you think there might be something to eat in one of these saddle bags?"

Frowning, he searched the sky. There were no hunting birds, only a few solitary larks. If they were going to stop, it was as well to do it now. He brought Cynfarch to a halt at the edge of a stream draped with willows. Dismounting stiffly, he helped Morgan down. The cool north wind rippled through the leaves above their heads and sent little waves lapping at the banks of the stream. Morgan shivered, hugging her arms to her chest, then dropped them self-consciously as she saw Arddu looking at her.

He shook his head. "You're going to *have* to wear my cloak, Morgan," he said.

"I'm not that cold. I've got my jacket."

"A garment made for an Earth climate," he pointed out.

"Earth's good enough for me," she said.

"Then let Earth's sun warm you!"

Silently she took the water pouch and went to fill it at the stream. Feeling a little ashamed of himself, he dealt with Cynfarch. The mare had been ridden many leagues that day, and seemed glad of a rubdown. He put the saddle back on at once in case they had to leave in a hurry, then checked and eased the harness. The horse stood aloof, tolerating his care, her intelligent eyes dark. Did she understand about Gwyar, Arddu wondered, leading her to the edge of the stream. While she drank, he gathered a handful of grain from the nearby field, then fed it to her.

"You want a drink?" Morgan asked, holding out the water pouch.

He shook his head. "Let's see if Gwyar left us anything to eat." He opened one of the saddle pouches. Morgan watched as he prowled through the contents, removing the things one at a time. Three small stones, oddly satisfying to the touch. A tiny bag of earth, rich and dark and with the smell of the island. A water pouch, still half full. Arddu went at once to fill it at the stream.

"What's this?" Morgan asked, pulling a round, lumpy object out of the bottom of the pouch. It was pale-green in color and lighter in weight than it looked. "Smells like food," she added hopefully.

Arddu almost cheered. "That's just what it is," he said. "Marroot's the best journey food there is. Are there any more?"

From the bottom of the pouch Morgan extracted half a dozen of the lumpy things. "Take a bite," Arddu told her. "Go on, you'll like it."

She obeyed cautiously, then made a surprised face. "Hey, not bad." It was a bit like potato, but with a cheesy sort of aftertaste. "The nicest thing about it is, it's not fish," she added.

"Not too much," Arddu warned her, as she took a second, larger bite. "It fills you up fast."

She passed the marroot to him, enjoying the comfortable feeling of decent food in her mouth, chewing longer than she needed just for the pleasure of it. She began examining the stones that had been in Gwyar's pouch, her fingers rolling them into patterns. Arddu took a couple of bites of marroot, then went to see what was in the saddle pouch on the other side.

To free it, he had to remove the long white bundle that was hanging over the pouch, tied by a strip of white linen. The thought of touching it made him hesitate, though he didn't know why. After all, it had been banging into his leg for hours. What was it, anyway? Gwyar had mentioned a sword. . . . He made himself grasp the narrow end. Nothing happened. He hefted it, looking at it curiously. A gleam of silver showed here and there through the wrappings. At the wide end the wrappings were even looser. Of its own volition, almost, his hand reached for that end and gripped it. And as his fingers closed around it a small patch of bare metal pressed into his palm.

Power surged into his hand, rushing through him like a tide. He yelped, prying at the thing with his free hand, but the metal stuck to his skin. *Get off me! Get off!* Knowledge winged through his mind, longing, hatred, rightness. What was it, gods, what was it?

"That must be the sword Gwyar wanted us to save," Morgan said from his side. "I wonder why —" And then, sharply, "What's the matter?"

Thoughts were flooding him, wild and impossible: possess, or be possessed; wield, or be wielded; mend, or be destroyed. It wanted too much! Violently he thrust the sword toward Morgan. "Take it!"

Astonished, she obeyed. It left his hand easily. She held it for a long moment, and her face went blank and cold, her thoughts shutting him out. At last she let the sword go, leaving it dangling at the end of the pommel. Neither said a word. White-faced, Arddu grabbed for the second saddle pouch, jerked it free of its tie, and stumbled away.

Keeping his back to Morgan and to the sword, he bent over the saddle pouch, pretending to have trouble with the knots. His hands were unsteady enough to make that true. What in the name of the gods had happened to him back there? He'd held a sword by its hilt, that was all. A sword: a linear, metal weapon. He'd grown up in the Circle, where such things were blasphemy. Maybe that was why. Gwyar herself had said it wasn't meant for the Circle.

But then why had she been taking it to them in the first place?

He rubbed the place on his palm where the naked sword hilt had touched. It burned as the hellebore juice had done so long ago on the island. Yet if he had had the courage, he would have picked up that sword again. He couldn't dismiss the feeling that there was something between the sword and him, a proffered kinship valuable above all things, if he could but deserve it.

"Do you need some help with those knots?"

Morgan sounded diffident, uncertain of her welcome. Gruffly he said, "Just finished." He didn't look at her, concentrating on the saddle-pouch. It was smaller and lighter than the other, but clearly not empty. As he drew it open, Arddu saw a silvery bundle streaked with black. He frowned, recognizing the colors of the Sisterhood. Gingerly he took the bundle out. It was folded in the shape of a broken circle, the circumference indented by a single jagged vee.

"What is it?" Morgan asked.

"A cloak, I think." He shook it out. It *was* a cloak, silver and black and deceptively light, a Sister's identifying garment.

He turned it over. Inside, on the hem, there were runes, written in something reddish-brown and crusty. With difficulty he read, "Elphin A'Vliant: her life-blood;" and something else, something about mountains.

Quickly he rubbed two bits of the hem together, effacing most of the runes. "Dirt," he said, pretending to brush it off.

Elphin, dead. That made two, counting Gwyar. Or maybe three? The vision he had caught from Rigan came back to him. Gwyar, Elphin, and Heledd on board *Kynthelig*, sailing to begin a war. Was this how they had begun it? Two of them dead, another disappeared, and only this cloak, and the sword, left?

He held out the cloak to Morgan. "Try it on," he said roughly. "It'll be warmer than it looks."

Morgan hesitated, then took it. With her back to him she slipped into the cloak. There was a long silence. "Well?" Arddu asked.

She turned, and his breath caught. In the silvery garment, her Earth clothing hidden, she looked so much like Rigan that he was unable to speak. She lifted her head, her fair hair and skin blending into the silver of the hood, her wide, steady eyes regarding him. "It is warm," she said then, but there

149

was a question in her voice. Did she guess she was wearing a Sister's death garment?

"You'll need it as we go farther north," he said, after a moment.

"How far are we going? What's in the north, anyway?"

"Legends," he said shortly. "You don't want to know."

"Why not?"

"Because you know too much already," he said. "Like about that sword, for instance. I saw your face when you held it. You know why Gwyar had it with her, don't you?"

She lifted her chin at him. "Maybe she was told the Circle would be able to use it. Maybe she was just — obeying orders."

"Maybe? Don't you know?"

"How would I know?"

"The way you knew about Rigan being Morgan LeFay? The way you knew we shouldn't use the horseshoe at Cwm Cawlwyd?"

She was glaring at him. He took a deep breath and tried again. "Morgan, this is important. An ordinary sword's all wrong to be a First Magic weapon. If the Circle did intend to use that sword —"

"All right! When I held the sword I thought maybe the Circle had sent Gwyar and the others after it because the Dreamer said it could destroy the Line."

There was an icy patch between Arddu's shoulder blades. "And the Dreamer saw us getting away on Gwyar's horse."

"So what?"

"She'll know we have the sword. She'll have seen the Line start after us. And even if Gwyar was right and there's some reason the Sisters can't use the sword themselves, they daren't take the chance that the Line will get it. The Circle will have to come after us, too."

Sickness rose in him. Things would have been bad enough with only the Line trying to capture them. But now what chance of escape did they have?

"The sword wants to go back," Morgan said.

"What did you say?"

"It wants to go back where it belongs. We've got to take this sword back."

150

The Line after them, and the Circle, and Morgan insisting on obeying a sword. He wanted to laugh, but it wasn't at all funny. "What we've got to do," he said, suddenly angry, "is save ourselves."

"Maybe the only way to do that is to save the sword."

"You can't know that."

"I can't know any of the things I do!" She was as angry as he was, now. "You listen to me, Arddu. This sword wants to go back, and it's a Magic. We've already got First and Second Magic against us. Do you want to have Third against us as well?"

"Third Magic? What are you talking about?"

"Don't act like you've never heard of it! You threatened the captain with it on the windsled!"

"That was just bluffing. The Old Magic on Nwm is long gone."

"Oh, yeah? What's the sword, then? You say it's not First Magic, and it can't be Second, or how could it destroy the Line? What else can it be but Old Magic, or Third, or whatever you want to call it? And what about the north? That's Old Magic, too. Why else does it have the Circle and the Line and everybody else on this stupid world so scared that no one even talks about it?"

He gaped at her. This was his world. He should have known. He should have been able to piece it together. Third Magic; the north; the sword. Why hadn't he seen?

"Maybe if we do what the sword wants, its magic will help us," she said, more quietly now.

"All right," he muttered. He couldn't look at her. "Which way do we go?"

"The sword will direct us."

He turned away. After a moment, Morgan mounted. He got up behind her, took the reins, and waited for orders. Morgan put her hand on the wrapped sword blade. "This way," she said, pointing. They started out.

Her silver-and-black hood billowed in the cold north wind. Behind her, hunched into his travel-weary brown, Arddu did what he was told. The sword gave directions, or Morgan did; it was nothing to do with him. He had become a passenger on this journey, and on this world.

151

SIXTEEN

And the three fountains there are,
Two above wind, and one above the earth,
May darkness and light bless thee!
— Black Book of Caermarthen X

THEY were lost. For three days now they'd had no idea of where they were. The horizon changed with every breath. Rivers they had crossed disappeared when they looked back. Mountains blinked in and out of vision, and forests they were sure they would enter in the next few minutes got farther and farther away. And at night, whatever well-hidden or sheltered spot they chose to sleep in, they would invariably wake to find themselves out in the open, in the middle of an exposed meadow ringed with hills and thick with flowers and bees.

They were unable to find out how this happened. Even when they took turns keeping watch, they both seemed to fall asleep at the crucial time. And when they awoke they would be in the meadow again, and in the distance they would see Cynfarch grazing near a fountain, white and tall.

It was morning, the sixth since they had passed the northern bounds of the Pwmpai. The day was even grayer than usual, the sky thick and cold with clouds, the distant fountain tinkling like ice. Chewing on some marroot, Morgan sat on the ground plucking the petals of a hardy flower, her eyes sweeping the sky. "No birds yet," Arddu said. "They never find us till we're out of the meadow."

"It's like some kind of game," Morgan mused, her fingers twisting and rolling the petals and laying them in a circle on the ground. "We follow the sword, the Line follows us, and

152

the Circle follows the Line, and somebody has to catch us before sunset or everything starts all over again the next day."

"It won't feel like a game if they do catch us," Arddu muttered. "And we're going to run out of food before we reach wherever it is the sword wants to go, if we keep coming back to this meadow every day."

"Maybe we aren't coming back to the same one. Suppose there are a whole lot of meadows, all just like this one, and we're being leap-frogged from one to the other? It would explain how the Circle and the Line lose track of us every night. Maybe it's the sword's magic keeping us safe and moving us forward at the same time."

"You don't think we're going in circles?"

"I'm sure we're not," Morgan said. "That sword's like a compass, always pointing north."

He got restlessly to his feet. He still had not touched the sword again. Six days, six long days with the sword giving directions and the land playing tricks and the birds closing in, all the time knowing that the sword was within his grasp, if only he dared . . . "Are we anywhere near where we're supposed to be?" he demanded.

She had plucked all the petals. Now she began shredding the leaves. "I don't know. The sword doesn't talk to me, not like that." Eyes downcast, she added, "And the sword's not the only one."

He knew what she meant. He didn't talk to her much these days. He didn't let himself listen to her thoughts, either. There was a barrier between them, and he didn't know who had erected it. "You don't say very much, either," he said defensively. "You sit there on Cynfarch and give the orders, but that's all."

"The sword gives the orders."

"You don't act that way. You act as if — gods, Morgan, this is my world, not yours!"

"Sometimes I'm not sure I've even got a world," she said. She reached for another flower, her fingers fretful.

"What do you mean?"

She didn't answer him for a long time. "When I was nine," she said finally, "I got really sick. My mother stayed with me

153

almost every minute; she even slept in my room. Sometimes at night I'd see her shadow on the wall, just hers, never mine." She looked at him appealingly. "That's what I'm feeling like these days, Arddu. I feel as if even my shadow has gone."

"What's happening to you?" The words were forced out of him.

Petals blew in the wind. "I don't know. I don't know."

"Tell me about your parents," he said, almost desperately. "Your mother, do you look like her?" Talk about them, he urged her silently, identify yourself with them, bring your own world back again!

"I looked a bit like her," she said after a long time.

"Look like her, you mean," he couldn't help saying. "Look, not looked."

"Is that what I mean?" She smiled almost painfully.

"What about your father? Are you like him, too?"

"He's got dark hair and blue eyes." She tore off another stem. "Do you look like your parents?"

"My mother was a servient. She's dead. I don't know who my father was." He shrugged. "Anyway, we're talking about your family, not mine."

She looked up then, scattering all the shredded flowers. "I'm not sure what we're talking about," she said. "Isn't it time we got going?"

And so they mounted up again, and between them the silence was as great as it had ever been.

★

On the seventh day they awoke, and the meadow wasn't there. They were in a tiny clearing in the thickest forest Arddu had ever seen. On either side, in front, behind, were trees growing so close together there was almost no undergrowth. The trees were old, their bark decayed and shaggy, their leaves rust colored. All around the clearing black branches hung low, nobbled with lichen and riddled with deep holes.

They scrambled to their feet. "Where's the meadow?" Morgan got out, her voice too quiet.

"I don't know," Arddu said. "Listen."

The wood was alive with rustles and creaks. Morgan and Arddu looked at each other, both suddenly very nervous. There was no room between the tree trunks for a horse. Their only possible route was a single narrow path angling off from one side of the clearing. It was very straight and very dark, easily the most uninviting forest path Arddu had ever seen.

"I don't like this," he muttered.

Morgan lifted up the white-wrapped sword from the ground beside her, where she had kept it while she slept. For a long moment she was still. Then she said, "We should go that way," and pointed to where the army of trees stood thickest.

"We can't. We'd never get through."

Cynfarch pressed up against Morgan, white flanks trembling. Morgan patted the horse, though her own hands were unsteady. "The sword hasn't steered us wrong up to now," she argued.

"You don't know that it hasn't. We could be anywhere. Anyway, whatever the sword says, we can't go to the right. Those trees are like a wall."

He went over and touched one of the trees at the right of the clearing. It was solid, definitely real. So was the one beside it, and the one beside that. He rapped his knuckles on them, to show her. Then he tried to wriggle between two others. His cloak snagged. "See?" he told her. "On foot we might get through. But we're not on foot. Are you prepared to abandon Cynfarch?"

"We can't leave her in a place like this. I guess we'll have to take that path. But as soon as the trees thin out we have to start following the sword again." Morgan chewed her lip anxiously.

Arddu saddled Cynfarch, more disturbed than he wanted to admit. Morgan began to hang the sword in its usual place. He watched her, the longing to hold it even sharper than usual. If only he could make himself, if only he didn't feel so afraid! Suddenly Morgan faced him. "I think today we'd better unwrap the sword. And we should keep it ready. We might have to use it."

He had not thought of it as a weapon. "I've never wielded a sword," he muttered uncomfortably.

155

"Neither have I," she said. She put the sword down so that she could mount. "Hand it to me, will you?" she asked, when she was in the saddle.

There was no reproach in her voice, not even any expectation. Shame filled him. Quickly he bent over, taking up the wrapped blade, offering it to her hilt-first. He hardly waited to see if she had it before scrambling up behind her. Her movements told him she was unwrapping the sword, but he wouldn't let himself look. With a violence he hadn't felt in a long time, he grabbed the reins, digging his heels into Cynfarch's flanks.

"Go on, Cynfarch," he said angrily. "Go!"

Morgan was looking at the sword. Unwrapped, it was a beautiful thing. The blade was silver, long and shimmering. The hilt was a coiling of reddish gold and silver, cables twined together like dragons. It had a rough-smooth feel to it, almost reptilian. Morgan stroked it, surprised how much she was drawn to it.

Cynfarch had been reluctant to set foot on the path, but her speed increased once they were on it. Trees met overhead, filtering the rusty light. They might have been riding through a tunnel. Other than the soft thud of Cynfarch's hooves, there was no sound. There were no birds, no animals of any kind. The sky, viewed in patches through the leafy canopy, was a uniform white, no sun, no moon.

Arddu looked back. They had not gone far, and had turned no corners. He ought to have been able to glimpse the clearing. But he couldn't. He couldn't even see the path. Trees brushed Cynfarch's tail. The forest was closing in behind them.

Thud-thud-thud went Cynfarch's hooves. Little puffs of dust swirled up with each step, vaguely chemical in odor. The path made a right angle to their left, then straightened again. *Thud-thud-thud*. Arddu sat higher in the saddle, looking over Morgan's head. The path again turned sharply left, and he saw a second path crossing the first, while the first divided into two narrower ones in a vee. Four possible directions.

"Which one?" he asked Morgan, pulling up at the intersection. Cynfarch was shuddering. He patted her absently.

Morgan's fingers were white-knuckled, curled around the hilt of the sword. "I don't know," she said at last.

"Doesn't the sword —?"

"It's stopped pointing the direction. We didn't go the right way when we should have, and now there is no right way. Arddu, we're lost!"

He sat stock-still. Thoughts rushed in, tales of a great northern forest, a maze of paths that led nowhere, paths a traveler must follow till he died of hunger or thirst. "Redynvre," he said aloud. "So that's where we are."

"We have to go back," Morgan said.

"We can't. The path's gone."

"I could wish us back," Morgan said. "I still have that one wish."

The horseshoe! He stared at her, wondering how he could have forgotten. "Get it out," he said, but as Morgan dug under her cloak he changed his mind. "Wait. Let's save it till we're desperate." Beneath him Cynfarch was shivering, transferring her weight from one side to the other. Suddenly she reared. Morgan almost fell off. Grabbing for her, Arddu leaned sideways. It was then that he saw. "Gods, look at Cynfarch's hooves!"

They were smoking. "They're burning up!" Morgan shrilled.

Without caring that there was no room, Arddu swung the mare to the left off the path. Cynfarch went gladly, shoving her way through a thicket, stopping only when she could go no farther. She was gouged with branches and bleeding, her eyes showing white. Arddu dismounted into the prickles, and with nervous hands examined Cynfarch's hooves. They were hot to the touch, the horny surface burned almost completely away.

"How is she?" Morgan asked anxiously.

"I don't know. She can't be ridden, that's certain. But since we can't go anywhere anyway —" Grimly he shook his head.

Morgan slid awkwardly from the saddle, one hand gripping the naked sword hilt, the other pushing branches aside so that she could stand. Almost with hatred Arddu looked at the sword. How beautiful it was!

"We should have trusted it," Morgan said, seeing his face.

"I should have, you mean. You think it was my fault."

"I never said that. But now that you've mentioned it . . ."
He jerked away, but she clutched at his sleeve. "You haven't
held it, not since the first time." She held it out to him. "Take
it, Arddu." Her voice was soft. "Take it."

It was so beautiful! His hands clenched and unclenched.
Then, desperate with longing, he grabbed it from her hand.

The world shifted.

Magic washed over him, and he let it happen. It was a
cleansing, a widening of the eyes, a healing. He had thought
himself a freak because he had the looks of female magic and
yet was male. A magicless boy whose birth had been without
meaning and whose life was without hope. A boy who belonged nowhere. But what he really was was Nwm, embattled
but still struggling. He was a fulcrum for the seesaw battle
between Circle and Line. He was balance, and he must survive.

Power was in his hand. Power *was* his hand. The sword
was his, and he was the sword's.

The waves of magic gentled. "Yes," he said. "Yes." And he
laughed, for the joy of it.

"Arddu?" Morgan said fearfully.

He understood her fear. How could he not understand?
She was so much like him! But he couldn't explain the delight
or the certainty; he could only feel it. Laughing again, he
hugged her, the sword bright and hard between them to help
her to see. But when he let her go she was still frowning. He
understood that, too. This sword was for him. She must discover her own pathfinder.

"It's all right," he said.

With the sword pointing like a wand in front of him, he
took Cynfarch's reins and began to find the way out of Redynvre.

SEVENTEEN

First to be satisfied is the pale one,
The eccentric.
— Book of Aneurin V

THE way was simple. It was merely to ignore all obvious paths, and to walk in the exact direction the sword indicated, whether that meant collision with a tree or not. It required faith. Sometimes it required desperately closed eyes. But as long as Morgan and Arddu listened only to the sword, they found a way through the trees.

Hours passed. Cynfarch was limping and white-eyed. Arddu was holding the sword with both hands, his whole body quivering with fatigue.

"The trees are thinning," Morgan said. "Look, there's a clearing. And there's a patch of sky over there. Arddu, I think the forest's coming to an end!"

They made their way to the clearing. It was nestled between a clump of pines and some bushes laden with golden flowers. The entire clearing was carpeted with fresh leaves. Some were green and some red, and they were all as supple as new skin. Everything smelled of wet, rich earth.

Before Arddu did anything else he made a nest for the sword from the linen rags that had once wrapped it, and laid it gently down. Then he took the saddle off Cynfarch, who was twitching with pain. While Morgan wiped the mare's steaming flanks, he examined the horse's feet, lifting them one after the other and muttering soothing words, but shaking his head over what he saw.

"She's hurting so much!" Morgan said. "Isn't there anything we can do? You know about herbs. There must be something that would help!"

He rubbed his neck, aching from the strain of holding the sword all day. "A bracken poultice would be good," he said. He put aside his tiredness. "I'll go look for some."

"I could do it. Bracken's a kind of fern, isn't it?"

"I'll go. You wouldn't know what to look for. It'd be better if you stayed and cleaned Cynfarch's feet. And . . . look after the sword, will you?"

A bit anxiously, she said, "Shouldn't you take it?"

He hesitated. The sword was heavy, and he was very tired. He shook his head. "There's got to be a stream near here; I can smell it. As long as I keep near it I won't get lost."

"Well, be careful."

He took one of the water pouches and left, looking over his shoulder before disappearing into the trees. Morgan had damped down a rag and was washing Cynfarch's feet. The mare allowed it, though another horse might have kicked out in agony.

Following the scent of water, Arddu pushed his way through a hawthorn thicket. Behind a copse of aspens he found a stream, bluebell-lined and heady with the scent of woodbine. He was out in the open, filling the water pouch, when he heard a loud *Cw-cw-cw*. He looked up and saw a cuckoo circle overhead, dark against the clouds. Then it darted off into the twilight.

So the Circle had tracked them down again. But there was nothing to be done about it, and Cynfarch had to be looked after.

He followed the stream, while evening deepened. He longed for the moon, but as usual the sky was too cloudy. The breeze was light but very cold, so he pulled up his hood. When he came to the dangling boughs of a large willow, he stopped short, knowing that a willow infusion would relieve Cynfarch's pain. With his sharp flint he scraped off some strips of bark and dropped them into the water pouch to steep.

As he worked, he caught sight of a large, brownish-green patch of bracken near a pond to his right. Quickly he finished what he was doing and headed for it. But the bracken was farther away than he thought, or he was more tired than he realized. What seemed a short distance took a long time. As he walked, the sound of water faded behind him. Ahead of him he became aware of a shadowy hump blocking the way. Arddu's nostrils flared with the sudden disgusting smell of rot.

Go back, his instincts warned.

He tried to turn, but something held him. He struggled, flailing his arms. It was no good. His feet felt as if they were tied to the ground. And then the shadow turned to confront him, and he saw that it was a female, and alive.

She was of monstrous girth, fat rolling on fat, her ancient features almost buried in waxy flesh. Her eyes made their own light, bright as twin moons. Despite her jarring size, she had a familiarity that horrified Arddu. He stood stunned, taking in the female's eyes, the scraps of fair hair draping the mushroom-colored brow, the incongruously clean, long fingers, the silver and black rags. Circle! his brain shrilled; but he knew that what he was seeing was something even the Circle would deny.

"What — who are you?" he croaked.

She began to hum, a cool, female melody, perilously binding.

He struggled to get words out, to stop that song of hers. "Are you . . . a Sister?"

Her tune broke off. "You have Circle looks," she said. "There was another such as you, once, a boy born when I was a Dreamer. I was not at his Testing. To keep that boy alive," she added, her voice sticky as honey, "another Sister must needs become Dreamer, and so I was displaced." Her lips were stretched back, showing teeth as sharp and white as a Linesman's. "There are compensations in the North, boy, but there are no *Kyntheligs*. I like you not."

Arddu choked. A long white index finger was pointing at his lips. "You will be silent," the Sister said calmly. "Come. See what awaits you, when I am finished my present entertainment."

His legs were like jointed stones, and would move only one way. He couldn't even turn his head. He began to move toward her. The smell made his stomach churn. When he was close enough almost to touch her, she oozed her vast bulk sideways, and he could see what her body had hidden. It was

161

a waist-high stone table on which sat a games board for Queens and Pawns, with a game in progress. At the other side of the table, panicked and wretched, stood a man in a flaming red cloak. He had a golden torc around his neck, and rubies on each finger. His hand was clenched around a red pawn.

A Linesman, Arddu thought in disbelief. But he could say nothing. He could not even blink. And neither could the Linesman.

"My entertainment," the Sister said.

She jerked her head, and Arddu's body was suddenly at the spectator's position at the table. Panting a little, the Sister maneuvered herself into place opposite the Linesman, where her head jerked again. The Linesman put down his pawn. His hand hovered desperately over his queen, then he reached for the pawn again and moved it one square. Held by invisible chains, Arddu had to watch. He had played the game often enough to know what its outcome would be. A red queen and a red pawn could never win against a full complement of black. The Linesman was doomed.

The man knew it, too. Arddu almost felt sorry for him. But all through the desperate suffering of the Linesman's next few moves, he never forgot the Sister's words. *See what awaits you,* she had said. His own turn was coming. Sooner or later, he was going to have to take the Linesman's place at that games board.

★

Morgan had cleaned Cynfarch's feet, given the mare a drink and rubbed her down again. Then, having done everything she could think of for the horse, she made a bed for herself in the soft leaves. Huddled there, holding a piece of marroot with one hand and the sword with the other, she watched the lengthening shadows and remembered a shadowy sickroom on Earth, and a little girl standing on tiptoe in the dusk with a pair of scissors in her hand.

Her father had brought her a gift that day. Morgan could see that gift as clearly as if it were still in front of her. It had taken a long time to unwrap, because the paper was too beautiful to tear, all golden and sparkly and covered with stars.

Inside was a tiny crystal unicorn, seeming almost to be made of light. Hanging over her bed, its facets had flashed out thousands of miniature sunbeams so brilliant and so lovely that Morgan had gasped in wonder. Dad had stayed only just long enough to give it to her. She had tried not to be pleased by the gift, because Mom was there and watching. But she had loved it, oh, she had loved it!

It was only after he had gone that Morgan had seen the depth of her mother's hurt. And when Mom had gone out to make supper, Morgan had stood on the bed, stretching as far as her nine-year-old arms could reach, and she had cut the unicorn down.

That had been one of the nights she had seen her mother's giant shadow on the wall, swallowing her own.

I wasn't choosing him over you, Mom. I would never have done that.

Methodically Morgan chewed her marroot and tried not to think. The food tasted like dust. Arddu had been gone a long time. She rubbed one damp palm into the silver-and-black cloak, then the other. The hem was turned upward. There were reddish-brown streaks on it. She ran the fingers of her left hand lightly over them.

In her mind she suddenly saw a face, beautiful and pale as death. *Beware,* the white lips sighed. *Beware Ysmere.*

In her other hand she felt the sword twitch. Slowly and heavily, she got to her feet. The sword was in both of her hands now, its weight dragging at her wrists.

"I'm going to find Arddu," she told Cynfarch.

The mare whickered softly. It was a warning.

"I can't help it," Morgan said.

When she left, Cynfarch was watching, head up and alert, and even the birds had stopped singing.

★

The Linesman was dead. Arddu had expected that, but he had not expected what came with it. Waves of sickness flooded him. He had been forced to watch the creature gorge. Abomination! And when she had done, the rubies and the torc and the desiccated carcase tossed, garbagelike, onto a mound in the trees behind the table, she faced him.

And for one terrible moment he thought she looked beautiful.

"You will play Red," she said. "I always give my opponent the advantage."

He felt himself tugged to the Linesman's side of the table. He had not seen her set up the games board, but all the pieces were ready. They sat there, the black ones shinier and thicker than before, the red seeming thin and fragile, like shells.

"Red plays first," she reminded him.

His fingers went out to the queen's pawn, the last piece the Linesman had played. It was still wet from the man's sweat. Arddu squeezed it in his palm, trying to think. Then, desperately uncaring, he moved it one square only, letting it sit. It was an unconventional move at best.

"So you prefer to lose quickly," she said.

He knew he wouldn't win, no matter what he did.

"There is such a thing as style," she said. She jerked her head at him, and he found that he had a voice.

"I have no intention of entertaining you," he got out defiantly.

Without removing her eyes from his face, she took a black pawn and moved it two squares. "Your move."

"No," said a new voice, "it's my move."

"Morgan!" Arddu exclaimed.

She was standing where he had first realized his own peril, stumbling into that nightmare game between the Sister and the Linesman. The Sister smiled, then turned slowly. Her body stilled, seeing the white face staring at her out of its black-and-silver hood, the tall, slim body lost in its enveloping cloak. No one spoke.

Finally Morgan said, slowly and firmly, "Your name is Ysmere. By your name I greet you."

Arddu's scalp prickled, so stony was the silence that followed. Then the Sister said, "I warn you, I have been without a name for so long that no name can bind me."

"But this is a small binding, a promise you may not even have to fulfil. I will play you at Queens and Pawns. If you win I will pay your price. But if you lose, you will pay mine."

"I never lose," the other said.

164

"But if you do, you will pay. That is the binding. By your name, Ysmere!"

A long moment passed. Then before Arddu's eyes the two pawns returned to their original position. He felt his legs taking him to the spectator's position once more. Morgan moved into place, keeping her cloak tightly around her. She did not meet Arddu's eyes, or even bother to look at the games board. Her eyes were locked on her opponent. And then she reached for her red horseman. Arddu cringed at the move, but it was too late. The game had begun.

★

Night was over. Games pieces littered the stone table, and more of them were red than black. But, astonishingly, red held the center of the board. The black queen was huddled into a corner, three of her pawns surrounding her, her horsemen scattered. Her two dragons were lost in a fork play, and two of her three warriors were blocked behind pawns. The red queen threatened, her horsemen attacking, a red dragon preventing black movement on two of the three available paths. Through bleary eyes Arddu watched, unable to believe what was happening, wanting to shout for joy and yet afraid to. The moves were obvious even to him. Red horse takes black pawn, red queen to the center, and Morgan would win. But there were still those two moves.

Neither of the players spoke. Morgan was waiting for black to move, and black was waiting for inspiration. A long time passed. "You have entertained me," said the Sister, raising her eyes at last.

"And you have lost," Morgan said.

"A game unfinished is not a game lost," said the other. Her hand brushed all the remaining red pieces off the board.

Morgan didn't even look surprised. "That was a dangerous move," she said, and threw back her cloak. Her hidden right hand swept the sword high in the air. Its glittering sharpness sang as it cut the air.

The other did not shrink, but her eyes were paler. "So that is what played me," she said. "I did not think it could be you."

165

"Still, you have lost." The sword hovered.

The light in Ysmere's eyes was terrible, sharp, and burning as a desert sky. "What price do you exact?"

"I demand," Morgan said slowly and carefully, "our immediate and safe passage with this sword to the land where it belongs."

The other lifted her chin. She might almost have been relieved. "To Yspyddadon, then," she said. "It will be done." Her long white fingers moved in the air. Clouds wreathed where her fingers had touched, a haze of magic surrounding Morgan and Arddu.

"*Our* passage, I said!" Morgan cried, still with the sword threatening. "I meant all of us! Cynfarch — our horse —"

"You did not say it," said the other. The magic was thicker now, a fog tugging at them. "The horse will be payment for your passage."

Her voice was thin, walled off from them by the fog, her body out of reach. But the games board was beneath them. Arddu wrenched the sword from Morgan's hands and smashed it down on the board, pulverizing the black queen and her retinue, sending stony dust screaming into the forest and the night. Beyond the fog a shriek was choked off.

"And that, Ysmere," Arddu said into the silence, "is my payment for Cynfarch."

EIGHTEEN

When extermination becomes the highest duty
From the sea to the shoreless land,
Say, lady, that the world is at an end.
— Red Book of Hergest I
(A Dialogue between Myrdin
and his sister Gwendydd)

ON a wintry mountainside, Morgan and Arddu clutched each other. Morgan was so angry she was almost crying. "Damn!" she said through her teeth, "damn, damn, damn!"

"It's not that bad," Arddu said.

"No? First I forget to include Cynfarch, and then I go and get us stuck up on a mountain. Why couldn't I have told Ysmere to send us to the exact place the sword belongs? But, no, I had to put in that bit about its land!" She sat down on the icy ground and rested her chin on her knees.

Arddu leaned on the sword, squinting into the distance. Away to the north he could see a faint glitter, like the glare of sunlight on glass. "I don't think we have too far to go. And at least you made sure we'd have the sword with us."

Morgan didn't even look up. "I should have made sure about Cynfarch, too."

"There's lots of forage where we left her, and a stream. In time her hooves will heal."

"Not if Ysmere gets to her first."

"I don't think she will." He was remembering how Ysmere's feasting had seemed to make the black gamespieces fatter. "I think Ysmere's magic was linked to her gamesboard, and that's ruined now." He wrapped both hands round the sword hilt. "How did you know her name?" he asked.

167

"Would you believe me if I said someone's face came and told me?"

"Why wouldn't I believe you? You have dreams all the time."

"Yes, well, this was different. The person who told me was dead."

He stared at her. "Dead?"

"She was a Sister. The one who used to own my cloak."

It was bitterly cold on the mountain, but for the first time since they'd left the Pwmpai the sky was free of clouds. In the east the sun was a blaze of white. Northward the moon was pale but clear. But under it the glassy glitter that had interested Arddu was dimming. "Fog's coming," he said. "We'd better get off this mountain while we can still see."

The way down was dangerous. Rocks that looked secure proved to be poorly balanced or slippery with ice. Now and then they would stare longingly at a sheltered valley lush with stands of larch and rowan, but they were following the sword, and it kept them to the slopes. By mid-afternoon they were numb with tiredness and cold. They quenched their thirst as they went, drinking the willow-tasting water meant for Cynfarch. It wasn't pleasant, but at least it took away their appetite. There was nothing to eat. All the marroot had been left with Cynfarch in the clearing.

Toward sunfall they disturbed a snowy owl perched in a nearby pine. Its white head swivelled, following them as they walked. After a minute the owl rose up, great wings flapping, then circled them a couple of times before flying off into the southwest.

"How does the Circle keep *finding* us?" Arddu demanded.

They started descending again. Below, fog was beginning to wreathe the valley, but the mountainside remained clear. When they finally reached the bottom of the last long slope, an icy mist was everywhere, and it was growing dark, too. "Hold onto my arm," Arddu told Morgan. "The sword will lead us."

They began walking, Arddu holding the sword with both hands. They followed it, stumbling with weariness. Suddenly they heard a cry: *Go Back! Go Back! Go Back!*

They jumped. "Grouse," Arddu muttered, with a shamed laugh, as the startled bird flapped almost into their faces. In a moment it was lost again in the mist. He took a few more steps. All at once the tension went out of him. "Gods, but I'm tired," he said.

"Me, too."

"If we roll ourselves up in both cloaks, we won't freeze."

"All right."

He lowered the sword. They passed the water pouch back and forth. Then, worn out, they curled up together on the hard ground and slept.

★

The mist was gone. High in the northern sky the moon was whirling, almost too bright to look at. Slowly and wonderingly, Morgan sat up. It was the deep of night, yet she could see great distances. The land was as livid as a black-and-white photograph taken in too much light. There were no trees. Bushes and grass were sparse, patched with large shiny areas where nothing grew. Were they lakes? she wondered. Away from the mountains the land descended slowly. In the north something needle-shaped and radiant seemed close enough to touch.

Morgan got to her feet, staring at the sharp, glittering thing. The glass giant. She wondered where the words in her mind had come from.

"What's the matter?" Beside her, Arddu scrambled up.

"Nothing," she said. "But look at that place, Arddu! Have you ever seen anything so . . . clear?"

He looked northward to that glassy glitter under the whirling moon. Unaccountably his heart lurched, his hand going automatically for the sword. It was tingling, or his hand was. A sudden urgency possessed him.

"We could make a good start if we left now. It's as bright as day now."

They walked all the rest of the night. When the sun rose the landscape grew so sharp-edged and clear it almost hurt the eye to look at it. The brilliant light made Morgan and Arddu very thirsty. Their water pouch was empty now, and there were no streams. The shiny patches Morgan had seen were not lakes, but large areas of once-molten stone so smooth and flat they might have been mirrors. These shone in daylight even more than at night. Morgan and Arddu had to pull their hoods down over their eyes to avoid the blinding reflections.

Over the hours the needle-shaped glitter ahead of them had grown. Morgan and Arddu were still some distance away, but now they could make out a tower sitting on top of a high, cone-shaped hill. The color of the tower changed with every step they took, winking now silver, now red, now black, now gold, a kaleidoscope that was as dizzying to look at as the circling moon above it. The sword pointed to it like the needle in a compass, dragging them along even as their feet flagged.

They rested at last. Arddu's sandals were wearing away on the sharp stones, and his feet were blistering. He stuffed strips from his tunic into the worst of the holes. The sun was westering, and a cold breeze from the north had sprung up. It carried a coarse dust that speckled them black, a grit that hurt their eyes and tasted bitter on their lips.

"Cinders," Morgan said, half to herself. She looked thoughtfully at the conical shape of the hill ahead. "I'll bet this whole place is volcanic."

"Volcanic?"

"That's when the underground stone gets so hot it melts and burns."

"Stone catches *fire?*"

She understood his horror. Stone was First Magic, and fire was Second. He had grown up believing such things were always separate. "On Earth it happens a lot," she said, trying to comfort him.

"Earth is Third Magic, then?"

"There's no magic on Earth. Everything's just science. The laws of nature, that sort of thing."

"The laws of nature *are* magic," he said firmly.

They went on then, lost in their own thoughts. Day passed into evening, and evening into night. They were too hungry and thirsty to sleep. Silently and wearily, they trudged on, following the sword toward the tower. Arddu never looked back, though now and then Morgan did. There was never anything to see, but in her mind, threadlike and perilous, female voices were calling her name.

★

The tower was three-sided and slender and made entirely of glass. It seemed too delicate to withstand the gritty wind. Nothing inside its polished, glittering walls could be seen. Now that the sun had set, the glaring reflections had become colorless, slashes of concentrated light constantly changing direction as the moon whirled. The hill the tower sat on was easier to look at, but even that was not the simple cone it had seemed from a distance. Under its age-smoothed surface, fires now extinct had sculpted it into a shape whose familiarity tickled at Morgan's mind. Four parallel ridges of white lava circled the hill, the top one crossed by a fifth, lumpier one that angled a short way downward. These top two ridges ringed the summit of the hill. It was there that the tower stood.

The wind had died at sunfall. By that time Morgan and Arddu were close enough to see that a circular lake surrounded the bottom of the hill. It wasn't a big lake. If it had been dry land, Morgan could have run across it in a few minutes. But she could see that Arddu was made nervous by it.

"What's wrong?" she asked, as they approached the bare, cindery bank.

"It's so . . . still," he replied. "There are no waves at all."

"It's a lake, not the ocean," she said. But she knew what he meant. Silvery in the moonlight, the lake was as smooth and fathomless as a mirror in an empty room.

"We're going to have to cross it to get to the tower," he muttered uneasily.

"If that's where the sword belongs, let's just do it, and not worry about it," Morgan said in a tired voice.

When she got to the bank, she stopped, gazing across the lake as she fumbled with the fastenings of her cloak. Suddenly her hands stilled. She stared at the hill rising like a clenched fist out of the water; at the tower, slender as a sword, rising out of that. Thoughts wisped through her mind, of kings mortally wounded and kings maimed, a land made barren, a midnight-blue cup. . . Her heart leaped. She knew what this scene reminded her of.

"It's a hand! Arddu, look! It's a hand holding the scabbard of a sword! It's just like in the King Arthur story, the hand rising out of the —"

"We're in trouble," Arddu broke in. He was facing the other way, and his voice was tight. "Look at that."

Morgan turned. He was pointing with the sword to a starless patch in the sky. "Birds," he said.

"It's still night," Morgan said stupidly. "Birds don't —"

But Arddu was already tearing off his cloak. "Why couldn't they have held off for just one more day?" He bundled up the sword. "Hurry!" he told Morgan. Then, holding his breath, he splashed into the water.

The water was hot! Staggering, he almost dropped the sword. He shouted a warning to Morgan, then blundered on. At least the lake was shallow, with a firm bottom. But hot water — gods! Magics melded in this land as if they had never been parted.

Morgan hurried after him, her cloak held high. The cloud of birds was nearer now, pasted against the white moon. She could see no sign of any human pursuers, but in her mind was the deep, cold murmur of female voices. She caught up to Arddu and they ran the last bit together, then scrambled up the underwater slope at the edge of the hill. With only her cloak to carry, Morgan was first, and when she found a level patch of dry land, she turned to give Arddu a hand.

For the first time she saw what they were running from. The searchlight moon outlined many horses, small as children's toys but running fast. She could see nothing of the riders; they blended too well with the moonlight and the dark. She shuddered. "Hurry," she whispered, "hurry, hurry." She didn't even know she was saying it.

Arddu clambered onto the level and shook out his cloak, freeing the sword. It glittered now almost as brightly as the tower, white light exploding off it in showers of sparks. He felt it urging him up the hill. He started forward, not thinking of Morgan, but she clutched at his arm.

"The Circle," she gasped. "Arddu, don't let them —"

Whose is the grave in the circular space?
She stumbled, her nails digging deep into his forearm.
"What's the matter?" he asked, the sword tugging and tugging.
Be the circle white or red?
"Morgan. Morgan!"
White or red, white or red?
"Neither!" Morgan suddenly screamed. "Neither, neither — both!"

On the other side of the lake, horses appeared, a huge knot of First Magic. They halted, cold and motionless, looking across the water at Morgan and Arddu. The silence was harrowing. Morgan began to quake. "I . . . I . . . ."

Desperately, Arddu pried her hand off his arm and placed it on the sword grip. Then he covered it with his own hands. The sword flared brighter and brighter. Suddenly, there appeared behind the Sisters a line of torches, red in the moonlight.

"The Line," Arddu said hoarsely. "Morgan, it's the Line!"

Across the water the horses reared and turned. Morgan slumped to her knees. Still with her hand between both of his, Arddu hauled her upright. Torches blending with moonlight, red with white, Circle with Line: gods, gods, what would come of this?

"Away from here," Morgan was whispering, "please, please, away."

He turned Morgan away from the sight. Then, half dragging her, he began following the sword up the ridged hillside toward the tower.

NINETEEN

Five zones of the earth, for as long as it will last.
One is cold, and the second is cold,
And the third is heat, disagreeable, unprofitable.
The fourth, paradise, the people will contain.
The fifth is the temperate,
And the gates of the universe.
　　　— Book of Taliessin LV
　　　(Song to the Great World)

B EHIND them, birds and horses were screaming. As they climbed the hill, Arddu imagined all the blood that would be pooling on that unabsorbing glass and cinder ground. Years might pass, and still that blood would remain, thickened and preserved by the cold into one unified pool. Whether it was First Magic or Second, blood was blood, and always red.

The sword was hot in his hand. Each step up the hill made it blaze brighter. "There, almost there," he found himself saying, whether to reassure the sword, or himself, he didn't know. Three ridges left. Two. One. They were at the top.

But there they had to stop. Even the sword dimmed a little. For a long, horrified moment, they could only stare. Between the hilltop and the tower was a moat of black water. It gurgled and frothed and spat steam and roiled, a boiling fermentation they dared not even think about touching. It was not very wide, but it might as well have been a league. There was no way across. They couldn't leap it and they couldn't swim; there was no boat and no bridge. The arched doorway of the tower was directly across from them and stood wide open, without even a gate. The tower needed only that moat to protect it.

Arddu couldn't believe it. The sword throbbed like a wound, insisting on the tower, desperate to reach it. "Maybe the water doesn't go the whole way around," he said.

They made a full circuit of the hilltop. The moat surrounded the tower completely.

Behind them the battle sounds grew louder. They tried to see what was happening, but with all the steam and the smoke of the torches, it was like looking through gauze. One of the Magics was winning. Arddu knew whichever it was would come after them. Yet he stood there, and Morgan stood there, and they didn't even try to escape.

There was nowhere left on Nwm for them to go.

★

Menw Line-End stood numbly on a tangled heap of red-cloaked bodies. In front of him a Sister, her cloak in shreds, was impaling herself on someone's discarded sword. He had driven her mad, even as the spell she cast had wound its way into him. *My last victory*, Menw thought. *I will not die alone.*

His limbs were heavy. Turning his head was an effort. Peering through the redness and the mist, he strove to make out another Linesman, even another Red Cloak. There was no one, only the dead. Owls called through the keening wind. The air was full of cinders.

The Circle had won a battle, and the Line was shorter. That was all that had happened. In Uffern no one would grieve.

No one would grieve anywhere.

But Menw, standing on that pile of corpses, felt a wetness on his cheeks. *I did not know that I could weep*, he thought. When there is only the self to live for, dying comes hard.

★

The sword pulsed in Arddu's hand. *I can't take you there!* he told it, but it wouldn't listen. It wanted the tower.

Sharp as broken glass, Arddu suddenly saw the answer. He could throw the sword across the moat, through the doorway and into the tower.

He didn't want to do it, so he tried for logic. The Circle must have gotten into the tower once before, to take the sword in the first place. What would stop them from doing it again? Or what if he threw short and it plunged uselessly into the moat? Besides, it would be stupid to throw away the sword now. Without it, he and Morgan would have nothing to bargain with, or to defend themselves.

Save the sword. It is what you came for. Save it.

Through the steamy night he looked at the moon, blazing with white light, and so cold.

We're going to die, anyway, he thought.

He didn't ask Morgan. He knew what she would say. One thing saved from disaster; not as good as three, but better, much better, than none. He ran the fingers of his left hand lightly down the blade, saying farewell. Then he hefted the sword like a spear, and let it fly.

★

On the other side of the lake, everything went suddenly still. For an instant the sky was divided by a ribbon of shining silver.

> *Fired from end to end, and splintered with ice:*
> *Who wouldst save me*
> *Mayst walk on me.*
>
> *Thou art my way,*
> *And I am thine,*
> *But not without cost.*

"Arddu!" Morgan exclaimed. She shook his shoulder violently, then pointed.

The sword spanned the moat, its grip on one side, its point on the other. It was much longer and broader, but still his sword — a sword-bridge crossing into the tower.

Arddu went down on his knees. His hand went out to the sword. The metal of the grip felt just the same. His fingers traced the coils lovingly. The blade had landed flat side up, and now was wide enough to walk on.

He stood up again. "Do you want to cross first?"

Morgan shook her head. Her eyes were huge. "Lancelot crossed a sword-bridge," she said.

Arddu put a foot on the sword. The bridge began to shimmer, and he knew there wasn't much time. He set the other foot on the sword as well, and slid the first one forward. "We have to hurry," he told Morgan.

Hurry, with boiling water below? Arddu was almost halfway across the moat now. If he could do it, she could. She made herself step onto the sword. The sweep of her cloak unbalanced her, and she teetered. She choked off a cry. One foot forward, then the other. The sword glistened ahead of her, wet with steam and shimmering so that she could hardly see it. Lancelot had crossed his sword-bridge on his hands and knees. But he'd cut his hands to ribbons doing it, and, anyway, it was too late now to change.

All at once she thought of the horseshoe. They still had one wish left. If she'd only remembered it sooner, they could have been across by now. From the mainland there came a sudden outcry. Voices now, female voices. Beneath her came the plop and splat of bubbles breaking. God, why hadn't she remembered the horseshoe? Why hadn't Arddu?

Ahead of her Arddu had reached the sword-tip. He stepped lightly off it into the glass arch, then reached a hand back to Morgan and pulled her to safety. "I heard Sisters," she stammered, clinging to him. "What are you doing?"

Arddu had let go of her and was bending over the sword. The shimmer had increased even more, an aura of lights and wispy shapes surrounding it. He grasped the blade, the tip resting against his palm. For a moment what he held was one end of a bridge. Then suddenly it was vibrating in his hand, its normal length again.

"Your hand!" Morgan cried out.

He blinked stupidly. The sharp point of the sword had cut away a circle of his flesh. Blood stained the silvery blade and dripped onto the glass floor. He went white, as much from shock as pain. The sword had done this!

My way, but not without cost.

He was still holding it by the point. Morgan took the hilt and put it gently into his right hand. Then she ripped a strip from the hem of her cloak and wrapped his wounded hand in it. The brown stain of Elphin A'Vliant's life blood mingled with his own, and the pain went away.

There was no time for wonder. Once again the sword had begun its clamor. "It still wants to go," Arddu said. "I can't stop it. I've got to —"

Morgan was straining her eyes back over the moat, but there was nothing to see. Everything was silent again. Had the Circle won or lost? Arddu was already hurrying through the tunneled archway. She ran after him. One after the other, like two shadows, they entered the tower.

★

There were no lights, only the moon. The tower was a labyrinth of passages separated from one another by thick walls and ceilings of glass. Ceiling upon ceiling rose above their heads, so many it was dizzying. Through the glass the moon seemed watery and distorted. But everywhere, no matter how deep in the tower they were, they could see its light.

Once, hurrying too eagerly, Arddu got ahead of Morgan. Turning a bend he saw her seem to approach him, facing him but in another corridor. They passed, he knocking on the wall to attract her attention, she deaf to him and blind. He made himself stop and wait for her, shouting nervously till she joined him. But he didn't go back. That much he had learned from Redynvre. To ignore the sword, to go his own way, would be madness.

Everywhere there were featureless, winding passages, linking and branching like nerves in a glass brain. Blind alleys winked at them from left and right, and grand stairways beckoned, but always they followed the sword. Once they saw fire, hot and red and far away, but the sword led them in the opposite direction. They came at last to a small staircase, rougher than the others, spiraling giddily through the ceilings above them.

"Here," Arddu said, and they began to climb.

Up they went, and up. Morgan began counting the steps aloud, but gave up sometime after four hundred. As they got higher, the stairwell narrowed so that there was scarcely room to sit. Tiredness was a lead weight within them, yet they went on. Now the stairs twisted tight as a corkscrew, and they had to use their hands to haul themselves up the slippery steps. They were lightheaded with hunger and fatigue, but there was nowhere to go, nothing to do but climb.

Up and up, Morgan's heart thudded, up and up and up.

Above them, a single layer of glass away, winged shadows covered the moon. Morgan craned her neck. Owls, she thought. The moon came out again, the owls moving on. Coming closer? Morgan dragged herself after Arddu.

There were voices in her mind again.

Almost there. It was a prayer. Almost there. And then, finally, they were.

At the top of the stairs was a door made of wood. Apple wood, Arddu thought, shoving with his free hand, trying to open it. It didn't budge. He stared at it in frustration. It was carved with strange symbols, an ancient rune writing that he couldn't read. Unnoticed, the sword in his hand brushed the door. It opened.

Pulled by the sword, Arddu crossed the threshold. For a moment Morgan was left alone, fighting the voices in her mind. The door began to close. Panic-stricken, she dashed inside, the closing door brushing her shoulder. She bumped into Arddu, and they both almost fell. When they had disentangled themselves the door was shut tight, and the voices in Morgan's mind were gone.

"The Circle's coming," she panted. Arddu was between her and the door, and she was facing him, not the room. He had a strange look. She tugged at his sleeve. "The Sisters know the way! The owls were watching us!"

"It's a spiral," he murmured, half to himself.

She turned to see what he meant. The chamber was a swirl of colors, black and red and gold and silver, the heart of a kaleidoscope. What it was made of, Morgan couldn't even guess. The room seemed huge, endless, even. The ceiling rose into the sky. Here it was not glass, but a deep, vaulted black, gold stars piercing it. The mosaic floor was studded with polished stone and bits of formed iron, making a spiral pattern that drew the eyes. Loop followed loop, wider and wider, spiraling away into eternity.

There was only one item of furniture in the room. It was a three-legged table standing at the center of the spiral. A piece of pink linen hid its top, covering three separate objects. Unaccountably, Morgan's heart beat faster.

Arddu started for the table. This was it, the place the sword belonged. He had got it here, and now it would leave him. A fierce pride raged against his misery and loss. *Thou art my way, and I am thine.* He reached out a hand and flicked the cloth away.

There were three things under the cloth: an ornate cup, a ring of stone, and a bodiless head.

And the head was freshly bleeding.

★

Arddu fell back, the tip of the sword ringing against the floor. Morgan's fingers were curved against her lips. The head was gaunt and hairless, and neither obviously male nor obviously female. It had wide, deepset, unwinking eyes of a strange, milky pink. The eyelids were pale and thick as beeswax, rising to the browbone. The mouth was stretched in a smile both merciless and kind. The neck was ragged-edged and bleeding bountifully. A small pool of red had collected beneath it; too small, for all that bleeding.

It looked very alive.

And then, slowly, the disturbing eyes swivelled.

It *was* alive. Morgan's breath hissed out. The head was looking at her.

"Sister," said the head, a thin, pale voice, high as a song.

She had to answer. "I'm not a Sister."

"Sister, Brother, First Magic, Second; verily, it is what thou must be. It is thy past and thy future."

"You're wrong." Defiantly, almost desperately. She didn't know what the head meant, but something in her sensed peril. "I'm not any kind of magic. I'm just me, just Morgan."

Arddu didn't understand, either, but he felt her fear. He went and stood close to her.

"I am the soothteller," the head declared. "I do not speak falsely. Child, thou art not just Morgan."

"I don't know what you mean!"

180

"Thou dost know. Thou hast known it for a long time."

Morgan stood, clenching and unclenching her fists. She couldn't say a word.

The waxy eyes turned to Arddu. "Sword-bearer."

Against his will, Arddu did not shrink away. He wanted to bow. He wanted, above all, not to look into those milky eyes. But the wide mouth spoke again, and he had to listen. "All thy choices have led to one choice, all thy roads to one road. Thy way, and the sword's: So hast thou chosen, so will it remain."

Arddu said uncomfortably, "I don't understand."

"Thine action at the moat bound the sword to thee. It is thine. It will serve thee well, if thou art true to it. But I tell thee, and I warn thee, it has a long memory."

And the wound in the jagged neck pulsed, and a great gout of blood splashed like a stone into the never-widening pool.

Arddu felt sick. A long memory. What did that mean? Suddenly he was afraid. By throwing the sword across the moat, by offering it its freedom, he had unknowingly bound it to him. Now it was his, and unless he would stay in the tower for the rest of his life, he must take it away from the only place in the world it wanted to be. Gods, what had he done?

"I'm not strong enough!" he protested. "I don't even know how to escape the Circle! I've been fighting it all my life, and haven't won yet. How am I supposed to manage the sword?"

"It is not by fighting the Circle, or the Line, that thou wilt escape them. It is not by fighting the sword that thou wilt manage it. Clearly there are lessons Nwm can still teach thee."

"I don't want any more lessons from this gods-forsaken world!"

"What doest thou want, then?"

He stared. No one had ever asked him such a question. But he knew the answer. He had known the answer his whole life. "I want to be free of the Circle and the Line," he said, "free of all the rules, free to find my own place!"

And the genderless voice rose and fell, a chanting song, funereal. "Freedom is acceptance. Freedom is balance. Freedom is the magic within thyself."

"The Circle looked inside me enough times and never found any magic," Arddu said. "Neither did the Line."

"The Circle looked only for Second Magic, and the Line for First. That is Nwm."

"Do you mean I have Third Magic, like the sword?"

The head's gaze was strange and unfocused. "Thou art the sword, and the sword is thee. Call it Third Magic if thou wilt. To me there is only one. Magic in the Sword, and the Stone, and the Grail, magic in the raven's wings, flying from this world, away and away. Let it go. Let it go. Let thee and thine go with it."

Arddu gaped. "Go? You mean, leave Nwm?"

"Verily, thou wilt leave Nwm." Tiredly.

"Arddu and I can go home?" Morgan cried joyfully.

"Thy former home is not for thee, not now."

All the color drained from Morgan's face. Even her eyes seemed white. "Not now? But sometime? Someday I can go home?"

"The Morgan thou wert will never go home. The Morgan thou wilt be may not want to when she must. Thou art changed, child. Thou wilt always remember too much."

"It's not fair," she whispered. "I don't deserve this."

"It is not fair, and it will not be easy, but there will be compensations. The Grail is one." The waxy eyes indicated the cup on the table. "Take it, child, and make it thine own. Thou wilt lose it, but something of it will stay with thee always."

The cup was exquisite. It had two handles, and a lining that was white as eggshells against the blue enamel of its exterior. Its rim was a band of pearls.

She had seen this before, she thought. Once, a long time ago, she had seen a thousand Morgans holding it in their hands.

Her hand went out to it, wanting it, but afraid. And from somewhere in her memory, like a ritual, she found the right question to ask. "Whom does it serve?"

A bell clanged.

The head rocked on its table.

Outside, on the glass tower, there came a patter of rain.

"Go," said the head. "Thy journey is as endless as the Circle itself."

"How do we —?"

The head intoned,

> "A sword with a sheath of stone: the way
> For journeying far, then back — to pay."

Sheath of stone. Suddenly Arddu knew. Eagerly his hand went out for the stone on the table. It was flat and round and had a hole through the middle that was just the right size for the blade of the sword. *A sword with a sheath of stone, the way.* A new world. No more Circle or Line. Freedom!

His gaze went to the head bleeding on the table. Guiltily he imagined it, alone when the Circle came. "What about you?" he asked it roughly. "Do you want to . . . I mean, should we take you, too?"

"Thou hast something of me inside thee already."

Arddu shuddered. He looked at Morgan. She had still not touched the cup. "The Grail," he reminded her, in a hurry to be gone.

Slowly, her hand moved toward it. The head watched impassively. "I don't want it," she said suddenly.

"Wanting is nothing," said the high, sad voice. "Only acceptance matters."

Still her hand hovered. Above their heads came another clang from a bell. "Hurry," Arddu whispered, feeling the sword reaching for the stone. The Grail was shining. Its beauty took the breath away. Morgan moved her hand closer, but still she couldn't make herself grasp it. Again, a third time, the bell clanged. Arddu couldn't help himself. He shoved the sword into the stone as far as it would go.

Morgan's hand clenched, convulsively, around the Grail. At last she knew what she had almost refused. She looked into its shining center and saw a glorious weaving of First Magic and Second, a union of people and dreams and fire and water, an unfinished panorama of which humanity was only a part. Morgan wept, recognizing that she herself was a thread in that weaving, inextricably linked to all the other threads, working with them, creating beauty with no knowledge of it and no freedom to refuse. But when through her tears she looked closer, she saw that she was more than just a thread, she was a weaver as well, using her own threads to weave the unique pattern that was herself. Her mother was one of those threads, and Arddu and Rigan; and Dad, too, Dad with the sunshine brilliance of his sea-blue eyes. For the love of her mother, she had rejected him as a thread; she had backed away from him all the while she had longed for him. It was as crippling as if she had cut away a piece of her body. She had woven herself twisted, and the radiant pattern she was a part of was less because of what she had done. Morgan wept again, for lost chances, for her father.

She didn't hear the sword singing in its sheath of stone. She didn't notice Arddu's shout of terror and joy. The kaleidoscope whirled, colors blending, pattern taking precedence over parts.

"We're going!" Arddu cried. "Morgan, we're going!"

His free hand clutched at Morgan's. A sea of magic swamped them. Their linked hands were the first to disappear, bones merging, blending with one another and with the magic. The sword next, then arms, heads, bodies, and legs. And through it all, until they were gone, the head watched and waited and suffered and bled. And not even Morgan with her Grail could have told if it was smiling or weeping.

TWENTY

And before they come,
The people of the world to the one hill,
They will not be able to do the least,
Without the power of the king.
  — Book of Taliessin XX
  (Song to Ale)

A RDDU opened his eyes. Overhead the sky was clear, a high, cold blue that had no moon in it. The wind smelled of rich earth and distant animals. He was sprawled on his back near a large boulder, his bandaged left palm resting against it. Why was it bandaged? He lay there, not moving, frowning at the moonless sky. His right hand was bent over his chest. Experimentally he moved it. It felt wrong, somehow. Empty.

Beside him, someone stirred. "Arddu?" He turned his head. A girl was lying curled on her side, facing him. There was another stone behind her, a body's length from her back. She was pale-eyed and pale-haired, and she had the saddest face he had ever seen. "Arddu, I've lost the Grail."

The Grail. Memory returned. A cup, enameled blue, standing on a table. A bleeding head, prophesying. A stone, flat and round with a central hole. Horses knotted on a lake front, torches advancing all in a line, blood spilling and pooling and thickening with cold. The glass tower, a boiling moat spanned by a bridge that was really a sword.

A sword with a sheath of stone, the way.

A sword.

With a cry he sat up. Frantically he pawed at his cloak and shook it out, though he knew the truth already. "The sword! Morgan, I've lost it!"

She raised herself to her knees. The sunlight made a nimbus of her hair. "You haven't lost it. Someone on this world took it."

On this world. He stared at her. He had forgotten. "We're not on Nwm," he whispered.

Slowly he got to his feet. They were surrounded by a ring of stones, nine of them altogether. The stones were unshaped and not very tall. They might have seemed natural, if they hadn't been so evenly spaced in a circle. Just outside the stone ring was ploughed land, rich and brown. Seedlings were pushing their way out of the furrows.

So it was spring, Arddu thought.

He looked instinctively for the moon to see where north was, before he remembered. "No moon," he muttered. How strange, and how difficult!

"There will be one," Morgan said. "You'll see it when the sun sets."

He frowned at her. "How do you know that?"

"And that way's east," she said drearily, pointing in the direction of the sun. It was yellow, and stood moderately high over a wooded horizon. "That's north," she said, pointing again, "and that's west." In both directions the horizon beyond the ploughed fields was the rich, unbroken green of forest. "And that way is south." This time he saw a patchwork of fields. Here and there were hut-type dwellings with conical roofs. On patches of green he saw moving dots that might be animals or people. A winding track led in the distance to a solitary hill. Away beyond that the horizon was the deeper blue of an ocean sky.

"The moon. All those directions. Morgan, *how do you know?*"

She looked at him in despair. "Can't you guess?"

Suddenly he could. "We're on Earth. This is your world."

"We're on Earth," she said with difficulty, "but, Arddu, it's not my world." Her face twisted, and she began to cry.

He didn't know what to do. They were far away from everything he understood, and his sword was gone, and the Grail, too. He looked southward toward that distant hill. It stood out against the sky, its ridged crown level except for marked notches that had an artificial look.

186

Thou art my way, and I am thine.
The sword.
It was there.

There was something else there, too. He went rigid, concentrating. At his side, Morgan had stopped crying, but he didn't notice, not even when he whirled to face her.

"I can hear her!" His eyes were feverish. "Morgan, Rigan's here!"

She looked at him tiredly. "Of course she's here. So is the M'rlendd, and so is Arthur. It's all coming together, don't you see? Excalibur was on Nwm. Someone had to bring it here. The sword in the stone. The hand coming out of the lake. All those legends had to have a start. We've brought them, you see? We're where it all came from. I suppose if we hadn't come, the legends would have started another way, and they would have been the same legends, they would have to be. But we did come, and so we're the cause."

"What are you talking about?"

"The only thing is, I don't know why we aren't in the legends, too."

"Morgan!"

She ignored him, scrabbling suddenly under her cloak. Then she drew out her hand, and in it Arddu could see the jade horseshoe.

"Why do I have this?" she demanded. "This horseshoe belonged to Rigan in this century. She had to have had it, or how else could she have passed it down our female line to me? But here it is, in *my* hand in *her* time! And two different people can't both have the same object in their possession, Arddu."

Arddu shrugged. "Maybe you're going to meet her and give it to her. Then she'll pass it down the female line and eventually you'll get it the way you should."

Morgan knew that was wrong. She couldn't be going to give the horseshoe to Rigan, because the horseshoe Morgan had inherited on twentieth-century Earth had had all three wishes intact, and this one had only a single wish left. Rigan must have handed down the intact horseshoe already, and fifteen actual centuries must have passed since the age of King Arthur. Yet here were Morgan and Arddu in the age of King Arthur once more! Time had circled back on itself instead of running on in a straight line. Which meant that all those centuries between the present and the twentieth century would have to be replayed.

Morgan shivered at the thought. So many years. Legends to be made and history to be kept exactly as it had been, and how was it to be managed, with her and Arddu here to mess everything up? There had already been changes. Bringing her horseshoe here was a perfect example. It would certainly have meant the immediate disappearance of Rigan's original horse-shoe, because Morgan had used the original one, and so that horseshoe with its three intact wishes no longer existed on Earth. Would it make a difference to Rigan? To history? She shivered again.

"Morgan, you're not listening! I want to know what you meant!" Arddu was almost shouting. "What was all that about Excalibur, and the legends, and us?"

"Let go of me!" He obeyed without thinking, startled by the power in her voice.

"Excalibur," she said coldly and clearly, "was King Arthur's sword. It was a magical sword he pulled from a stone. And you brought it for him, Arddu. Excalibur is your sword."

★

The high king lay on a bier in the House of the Dead. The cries of mourners rose like smoke through the roof hole. In a partitioned antechamber, lesser kings drank their mead and eyed each other suspiciously. Outside, the hill fort was crowded. All day, people and horses and oxen and pigs had been flood-ing through the main entrance. Some were strangers from the east, driven westward by the Saxons. Others had come for the next day's funeral. But most were here for the succession. The high king was dead, and he had no heir. Someone must take over, or there would be division when the Saxons came. No one knew who the new high king would be, and everyone was afraid the decision would be a bloody one.

Inside an isolated meeting house, five of the dead king's advisors stood in a ring around a table. It ought to have been dark in the room, with the steep thatched roof blocking the sunlight and the solitary door tightly closed. But the Council had lit no torch. For on the table was something that shimmered so brightly it made its own light.

It was a sword, its silver blade tapered and shining and incredibly sharp. The hilt was a mixture of metals and colors, gold and silver serpents twining together in enigmatic union. Where the hilt and the blade met was a ring of stone like a collar, rendering the blade useless.

Silently, in turn, each of the five men took hold of the tight-fitting stone collar and tried to remove it. "Did I not say it was impossible?" a sixth man said, near the door. "This is no ordinary sword. Anyone can see that."

"Where did you find it, peddler?" asked another, an old man in white robes.

The peddler held out his palm. With contempt, the old man opened a pouch and tossed a coin in the direction of the door.

"In the Stones." The peddler's voice was muffled, as he reached for the coin.

"Was there anything else there?"

The peddler licked his lips. "No," he said.

"You are a liar."

"I tell you, that sword was just lying there, all by itself in the Stones. It came by magic, I can see that now. The Stones knew our high king had no heir. And . . ." He licked his lips again, clearly working it out as he spoke ". . . and so they made that sword and put the collar around it, so that whoever pulled it free could be our next king."

"Liar!" the first man snorted.

"Throw him out," someone else said.

"A single coin, for a magical sword?" the peddler shouted angrily. "Is our new high king not worth more than that?"

"Give him ten," said the old man.

The door opened and closed. "He will put that story to the world," said a man who had been quiet till now. "There will be some who will believe him."

Slowly the old man reached out and touched the shining blade. "Perhaps it is not a bad idea."

"What are you saying? That we should actually allow whoever can pull this sword from its collar to be our next high king?"

"I am saying," the old man said oddly, "that truth comes in strange colors, and even a peddler's lies can be prophecy."

"But what if no one can free the blade?"

"Then combat must choose the successor. But if someone really can free this sword from the stone, let him be our next king."

And another man, who had said not a word until now, rubbed cold hands beneath his robe and said, "Then, please, God, let him not be a Saxon."

★

The M'rlendd was on his way to the hill fort. Behind him on the crowded, noisy path, Arthur was leading the donkey. The boy's silence was unnatural, setting him apart from everyone else come to witness the succession. Did he guess what the M'rlendd had in mind for him? The boy was ready for kingship, though the M'rlendd might have wished him a few years older. These Earth people would find it hard to accept a fifteen-year-old as their leader. But two nights ago there had been a red ring around the moon, and the king had left no heir. There was no doubt in the M'rlendd's mind that this was Arthur's time.

The road to victory, the M'rlendd thought, and wondered why it seemed so flat.

Somehow, he had expected it to be harder. Oh, yes, there had been the Morrigan. How he had enjoyed spiting her, making her watch his own Second Magic taking control of the island and the cave and, eventually, of Arthur as well! Most satisfying of all had been those few moments with her unwilling body. He had bested her then, and in a way no Linesman had ever managed with a Sister. He had expected to have to fight for his life, afterward. He had not expected her simply to leave the island and never come back.

All these moons with no sign of her, yet never once had he relaxed his mental guard. Shielded, he was too strong for her to Spell his death. But First Magic was known for its patience.

She would wait for the right time, and then she would seek her revenge.

She might even be here today. He took off his cloak and turned it the wrong way out. In so crowded a place, the first he might know of her presence might be a flint knife slipped unnoticed into his scarlet-identified back.

In the hill fort, the M'rlendd heard about the sword again and again. ". . . made of magical metal, sheathed in stone," said one voice, awed. And another, "They say — did you hear? — whoever pulls the sword from the stone will be our next high king."

The M'rlendd glanced at Arthur, who was silently tethering the donkey. The boy's young, secretive face remained expressionless, but his eyes were alight. Within himself the M'rlendd smiled. Ambition, he thought. Oh, yes, Arthur has learned this much, at least, from me.

★

Across the enclosure, the Morrigan wandered through the crowd. She had a baby slung from her neck, leaving both arms free. Long ago she had stopped using dye on her hair, and beneath her ragged hood her hair was nearly white. No one gave her a second glance, or noticed the defiance that was all that was left of her beauty.

Now and then the baby would let out a cry. "Quiet, Mordred," she would say, without looking at it. "Your father wouldn't approve."

And in his sling Mordred would give his mother the blue gaze that usually made her quail, but now she did not even notice.

The Morrigan had much on her mind. She had not yet discovered the M'rlendd, or Arthur. But they were here, she knew it. Her eyes searched everywhere for them.

She knew what she was going to do. She patted the packet she had sewn into her tunic. She had checked it just before entering the hill fort, and been reassured by the small, hard thing it contained. But this time she felt nothing. Her heart flew into her throat.

Frantically shoving the baby's sling to one side, she felt for the threads of the packet. They were still intact. The packet was there, sewn up tight. The thing it contained couldn't have disappeared. She forced her hands to steadiness, and unpicked the threads. The packet tumbled into her hand. She unwrapped it. It was empty.

She might have screamed. For a moment she thought she had. Gone. Gone. The half-circlet was gone.

She had nothing of Nwm left.

★

"You won't be able to get it back," Morgan said. "Arddu, the sword *has* to go to King Arthur! I've told you and told you, it's the way Earth history turns out!"

"I don't care how Earth history turns out," Arddu said, grimly shouldering his way through the people ahead of them on the track. "It's my sword."

They were almost at the top of the hill. A wall of earth fortified the summit, surrounded by a deep ditch. The main entrance to the hilltop enclosure was a gap in the earthen wall, where a wooden gate stood open. A causeway like a bridge of earth led over the ditch to that gate. A pair of men wearing short, hooded cloaks guarded it. They frowned uneasily at Morgan's coloring and strange clothing.

There was a sudden shout from inside the enclosure. "The sword! They're going to test it!"

Like a wave crashing on a beach the crowd surged toward the meeting house. Even the two guards at the gate turned their heads to look. In the uproar Arddu and Morgan entered the city unchallenged. But a huge throng lay between them and the meeting house, and they could see nothing. Only the cheers of the people told them when the dead king's councillors and their warrior guard came out, bearing the sword. But Arddu would have known, anyway. The sword called to him, and he couldn't get to it. He pushed desperately through the crowd, pulling Morgan behind him.

In the testing ground, one set of hands after another was grabbing at the sword, yanking at the stone collar, trying to release it. No one succeeded. "Cunos's turn now!" Arddu heard, and, "If he doesn't free it, no one will!" Then cheers and roars and a disappointed hiss, followed by renewed cheering as other hands took over. At last a boy stepped forward. "Allow me!" he commanded, his voice young and confident.

The people looked at the boy, a head shorter than the warriors who had been unable to budge the stone, and their laughter rang out. Arddu's heart thumped. This was Arthur, the boy he'd seen in Morgan's mind, the one she had said would be king. Suddenly there came a rush of sound, a withdrawn breath from all who could see. "That's the magician, Merlin — there, turning his cloak the other way. He's going to speak for that boy!"

And then, from a voice thick with Second Magic like the heat of a Nwm desert, Arddu heard, "People of Britain, you see before you the only person who can release this sword from the stone. Britons, look on Arthur, your Once and Future King!"

TWENTY-ONE

In the deep, below the earth,
In the sky, above the earth,
There is one that knows what sadness is,
Better than joy.
> — Book of Taliessin VII
> (Hostile Confederacy)

"HE'S going to get it out," Morgan was wailing. "Arddu! It's going to be his!"

He shook her off, elbowing people out of the way. In the testing ground the M'rlendd was moving back, his cloak bright as fresh blood. Now the boy Arthur was bowing to the Council; now he was holding the sword high overhead. Reflected sunlight dazzled off the narrow sword tip, but the heavy stone collar at the hilt end of the blade looked black and ominous. While Arddu battered his way closer, Arthur began whirling the sword around his head. It seemed an impossible task for so slight a youth, but slowly his speed increased. Around and around the sword whirled, faster and faster and faster. The air whined shrilly. The boy's grim determination was evident in every muscle of his body. Arddu could see his expression now, the longing to find his own place, to be his own person. *I know you*, Arddu thought suddenly. No mother and no father, only Rigan to love, and Second Magic waiting outside, hungry. *I know you.*

All at once, the boy was stronger. The sword whirled, brighter and brighter, a harmony of silver and red leaving visible light spiraling in the air. Arddu knew there was magic here. And it wasn't just the M'rlendd's.

Rigan!

Mind to mind he reached for her. A woman at the front gave a startled jerk, then slowly turned to face him. Out in the testing ground the sword whirled less strongly.

Rigan was wearing the clothing of this world, skirted and ragged. Arddu was shocked how old she looked, how ruined.

Arddu, her mind said. She didn't smile. *I thought the Line had taken you. How came you to Earth?*

No happiness to see him, Arddu thought. He lifted his chin. *That sword brought me. It's mine, Rigan. It's Third Magic, and it's bound to me, and that boy out there cannot have it.*

Her brows went up. *Where would you find something that is Third Magic?*

Gwyar gave it to me. She and Elphin and Heledd went into the north to find it. They intended to destroy the Line with it, but Gwyar realized —

North? Don't lie to me! Gwyar and Heledd and Elphin were going east to arm the windports. That was how the Circle intended to destroy the Line. There was never any question of a sword.

I'm not lying, Rigan. Look into my mind. You'll see.

The boy in the testing ground was really struggling, now. People were cursing him or shouting encouragement. But Arddu was watching Rigan. Suddenly her shield slammed up like a barrier of ice.

"So it was my Sisters who lied," she said, loud and conversational, across the heads of four people. No one was listening. Everyone was watching the boy with the sword. "Was it to test me? Did they think I would betray them? All these years. All this."

There was nothing but conversation in her voice, but briefly Arddu was terrified. "Don't make that boy into a king, Rigan. Why should you give the Circle an Earth leader, or anything else? And why help the M'rlendd? Second Magic won't be able to get the sword out of that stone. But First Magic working with Second — the boy will be king, and he'll own the sword, and — gods, Rigan, don't do it!"

She smiled queerly. "Why should he not have what he wants, for a moment or two? Why shouldn't the M'rlendd?"

Somewhere a baby began to cry.

Like shattering glass her shield broke. Anguish swept from her mind into his. *I had a jade circlet once, and it was divided. I hoped to mend it, and the pieces disappeared. I found the sea serpent's egg, and Arthur smashed it. I had Sisters once, and a world, and now I find they were never my own. Let the M'rlendd know what it is to have hope destroyed! Let Arthur know what it is to lose something he has already grasped!*

She turned her back. In the testing ground the boy had the sword whirling again, faster and faster, magics whirling with it, Circle and Line connecting, fusing. . . . Something small and green dropped from his flaring cloak. No one noticed. The sword was a whirling blur, its magic mesmerizing the crowd. A sudden hush fell.

No! Arddu's mind shouted. *It's my sword, not his! Rigan, stop!*

He flung himself into the testing ground, but it was too late. With a grate and a creak the stone collar whirled off the sword tip and flew through the air, thudding at last into the ground almost on top of an abandoned baby.

★

Arthur was holding the naked sword upright, waiting for acclaim. But the crowd remained silent. Only one person spoke. "So, Arthur," the Morrigan said, entering the clearing, "so now you are king." An unearthly white light shrouded her. No breath, no movement disturbed the still air.

"Rigan?" It was Arddu. He had stopped short, halfway between the M'rlendd and the Morrigan. There was something in his sister's face. . . . "Rigan, what are you going to —?"

She paid him no heed. "Do you like it, Arthur? Are you enjoying the fruits of all your deeds?"

"You never cared about me, Morgan," Arthur said. His voice was shaking. "I didn't do anything that you wouldn't have done to me, in time."

Arddu felt blackness thickening in his sister's mind. Now he knew what that look on her face had meant. Icy-cold, he shouted, "Rigan. Don't do it. Rigan!"

The Morrigan tilted her head. She might have been listening. But her silver eyes saw only her own hands over the abyss and Arthur hanging from them. A young Arthur, smiling joy-fully into her eyes, trusting in her.

But he had chosen the M'rlendd. He must pay. And in his paying, the M'rlendd would pay also.

"You will never be King Arthur," she told the boy coldly, and her eyes went as black as the thing in her mind.

The boy's face twisted in agony. The sword was still high in the air, impotent in his hands. Blood spurted from between his fingers. He didn't make a sound, but Arddu heard scream-ing. He realized it was himself.

"Rigan, it's wrong! Stop!"

She would not stop. Arddu leaped at her then, pummeling her with his fists. She fell back, surprised by him, then shook herself free. Falling, Arddu touched her mind with his. He drew away in horror, sucking in his breath. Second Magic was in Rigan's brain, burning away at her reason. She wasn't even trying to fight it. All she cared about was what she was doing to that boy.

Arthur was cracking like ground in an earthquake. Blood fountained from his mouth. He choked and retched around the awful torrent, but couldn't even wipe it away. It was obscene. Arddu wanted to vomit. *Rigan, don't! Please, don't!* The sword was dulling in the sky, dying like Arthur. Tears poured down Arddu's cheeks, down Arthur's. There was only one way to stop her. Arddu ran to Arthur and threw his arms around him, shielding him from Rigan with his own body.

She would stop now, she must. He was Arddu, he was her brother. She had always protected him.

But Rigan looked at her twin and saw only herself, and her eyes remained black and hot as a night in Bryn Tyddwl.

★

The M'rlendd was walking away. The power of Death was not his to wield, but it didn't matter. He had destroyed the Mor-rigan. He had maddened her, and she had done the forbidden: she had used the magic of Death on an innocent, her own brother. No magic would ever help her again. The Morrigan was finished.

But the sword would remain. When it was all over, someone there would pick it up. Possessing it would make that person a leader, someone who would be easily won over to the Line's purposes, now that there was no First Magic left on Earth to compete.

The M'rlendd smiled to himself. By the gods, could it be easier? A little time had been lost, that was all. When eventually he went home to Nwm, it would be with this wretched world under Line control, and with the destruction of a Sister to his personal credit. He would be sure to move up in Line. It was all highly satisfactory.

★

"Arddu!" Morgan shrilled.

She had been too far back to know what was happening. Freed of the crowd at last, she saw Arddu throw his arms protectively around the other boy. Then both boys fell to the ground, stunned and bleeding. A woman who could only be Rigan was staring ominously at the two unprotected bodies.

She was killing them!

"Stop it!" Morgan shrieked.

But Rigan didn't stop. In front of her eyes the boy Arthur turned slimy and dissolved. And Arddu —

"No. No!"

Arddu was motionless, bleeding from his eyes and mouth. The sword was near him on the ground.

Sobbing wildly, Morgan ran toward Rigan. "How could you? He loved you more than anything. He was your brother!"

Slowly and rigidly, the Morrigan bent over and picked up the sword. Then she turned, and Morgan saw herself, older and destroyed.

"I loved him, too," Rigan said, "but one of us should never have been born. I wish it had been me."

She didn't question Morgan's presence, or the black-and-silver cloak, or the face that might have been her own. "I have found my punishment," she whispered. She had the sword in her hand. She lifted it high in the air, and it caught fire in her hand.

"Bring him back!" Morgan cried to her. "Save him!"

"I cannot. My magic is gone." And in her hand the sword flared brighter, and her skin began to peel.

Pain, so much pain. Morgan flung herself onto Arddu's body. She was sobbing as she ran her hands down his arms, his face, feeling for life. There was no movement in his chest. She buried her face in his ragged brown cloak. "It's all so wrong," she cried. She tried to lift him, to make him sit up. "I haven't anybody. Arddu, I need you!"

He would not sit up. He would not breathe. Under his back her hand made a fist around a small, hard stone that lay there, gripping it like a lifeline.

"Arddu, don't be dead!"

But only silence answered her, and the smell of burning. She turned her head, tears pouring down her face. The Morrigan's hand was on fire. Slowly, Morgan's fist moved to her lips. She pressed it there, holding in the scream that was bubbling inside. The smell of burning was like a sickness.

So this was how it was to end. King Arthur dead. Arddu dead. Morgan LeFay on fire. The legends ruined beyond repair.

"I don't know what to do!" Morgan wailed suddenly. "Rigan, tell me what to do!"

And in her mind, suddenly, she knew. Her fist opened, and she looked down at the stone she had clutched up from the slime that had been Arthur, and it wasn't a stone at all, but a small green semicircle of jade.

With her free hand she reached into her pocket. Her horseshoe was there. She pulled it out. One on each palm, she looked at them. They were two halves of the same whole. They were meant to be together. She looked up at Rigan, and saw her own eyes looking back at her in torment.

"Do it now," Rigan got out, "please, Sister, do it now."

Morgan closed her eyes and let the words form themselves from her soul. *Make things the way they ought to be*, she wished. *Please, oh, please, make things right.*

And then, blindly, she brought the two halves of the circle together again, and the world changed.

★

She opened her eyes to the sound of cheering. She was standing in the testing ground. Laughing people were surging forward. There was no sign of the Morrigan or Arthur. But a smiling Arddu was there, sweeping Excalibur through the air to the delight of small children. With shining eyes, Morgan looked at him. Not dead, after all. Not dead!

"Arthur!" the people cried to him, getting his name wrong. But it was the only name they knew, the only name the future would allow. "All hail Arthur, the Once and Future King!"

He raised a hand for silence. "And this is my beloved sister," he said, throwing his free arm around Morgan's shoulders. "This is Morgan LeFay."

She lifted her eyes to his face, but he was grinning at a little boy and didn't see. And then people were cheering Morgan, too. "Hail to the sister of Arthur! Hail, all hail, to Morgan LeFay!"

As if in a dream Morgan waved to them and smiled, doing what Morgan LeFay would do, making them happy.

A small solid circlet of green jade was dull in her hand.

Make it right, she had said. And so she had become Morgan LeFay, and Arddu had become King Arthur, and the legends were there, waiting to be made.

For Arddu there was kingship, and all the choices that would lead, in the end, to the breaking of the Round Table and death on the battlefield. For her there was a Quest to be initiated and a sorcerer named Merlin to be bested, and above all, there was a baby named Mordred to be kept alive. For without that baby, Morgan Lefevre would have no ancestors, and without ancestors, she could never be born. And she must be born, for she was here now.

And so Mordred must live to kill Arddu, and she, who loved Arddu, had no choice but to allow it.

And Morgan smiled and waved and smiled again, and her throat was tight behind her smile, and her heart longed for the days when she had had choices, when she had been just Morgan, just herself.

Thou hast changed, child. Thou wilt always remember too much.

Where had it happened? On Nwm, when she had known things she should not, the things a Sister would know? On twentieth-century Earth, seeing the Grail reflected in the window of an inn? Here, bringing the Morrigan and herself together like those two pieces of jade? Who was she, really? What was she?

And from the Grail that she had lost, from the part of it that would stay with her forever, came the answer.

Thou art the daughter of First Magic and of Second. Thou art thy father and thy mother. Thou art the link that bends the line. Thou, Morgan LeFay, Morrigan, Morgan Lefevre, art the lesson of the Third Magic.

The crowd was thinning. Arthur was surrounded by lesser kings and children. Away near a scrubby thorn bush, a bundled-up baby was wailing, all on its own and ignored. Slowly Morgan made her way toward the ragged bundle. It had stopped crying by the time she got there. Bending over, she saw something hard and round lying beside the baby. It was the sword's stone sheath.

Morgan stared at it for a moment, wondering and unsure. A high, clear voice seemed to whisper in her mind.

A sword with a sheath of stone, the way
For journeying far, then back . . .

Back. In a flash she saw it: herself on a raven-strewn battlefield taking Arddu's dead body in her arms and then thrusting his sword into this same flat, holed stone, taking them both back to Nwm.

So that was the source of the legend of Morgan LeFay taking the dead King Arthur to be reborn in a magical land! Amazed and joyful, she let full realization come to her. Arddu's death at Mordred's hands would not last forever. There would be life on Nwm afterward, years and years for herself and Arddu, years when she didn't have to know the outcome, when she might make choices. She must be Morgan LeFay until then, but afterward — oh, God, gods! — she could be herself.

She picked up the stone, putting it deep into the pocket of her black-and-silver cloak. The blue-eyed baby watched her, whimpering a little. He was hungry. And she looked at him, at that child of First Magic and Second, at the Morrigan's baby who was now her own, and suddenly she pitied him. "Poor Mordred," she said, "you can't help it, either, can you?"

And lifting him into the circle of her arms, she went to find him some milk.

EPILOG

And to us then there shall be a relief after our ills,
And from generosity none will be excluded.
— Black Book of Caermarthen XVIII

WAVES rolling, a soft hiss against the stony shore. Seabirds wheeling above the dunes, crying to the moon and the sun. The trickle of the River Ffraw, endlessly losing itself in the sea.

"At least Cwm Cawlwyd has not changed."

"Everything changes, Arddu." Morgan pointed to a ship anchored offshore. It was not the *Kynthelig*. The wind blew her hair into her eyes. It was white now, not just fair.

"You insist on doing this?" Arddu asked. His lips were thin with strain. "You will not change your mind?"

"I will not."

"We've been together so long, Morgan."

"Nwm, Earth, Nwm again . . ." She smiled painfully. "Why did we always forget the last part of the head's rhyme?"

He scrubbed angrily at his eyes. "What if the Sisters refuse to mission you? What if they're still so angry they —"

"They will mission me. They'll be happy to get me out of Nwm forever. Besides, they know it is what must be. There is a child on twentieth-century Earth who must be born."

"And when she grows to the age of fifteen and her father takes her to Tintagel, there will be no one on Nwm who will summon her, Morgan. It is forever, this goodbye of ours."

"Do you think I don't know that?" she demanded, suddenly fierce. "I'll be born knowing it! And I'll never forget it, not when I'm fifteen, not when I'm a hundred and fifteen! Look at me, Arddu. Do you really think I want to do this?"

She was weeping. He put his arms around her. For a time they were silent. At last he said hoarsely, "It won't be easy for either of us, but there will be — compensations."

They kissed. Then Arddu held up his hand, scarred on a sword bridge years ago. "Every time I look at this, I will remember you tearing off the hem of your cloak to bandage it." He touched his side, where Mordred's sword had cut deep. "I'll touch this, and remember how you brought me to Nwm again, and healed me."

"I don't know if I want to be remembered by a bunch of aches and pains!" She tried to laugh.

"And arguments, too; don't forget all the arguments!" He, too, was trying. Suddenly he hugged her, then brushed her eyes with his lips. Without another word he went away.

A long time later Morgan lifted her face into the wind. The endless blue ocean dazzled, glints of lights dancing in the rainbow-colored froth. She stared out at it, at that glory of water lit by the sun and the moon, and suddenly she felt at peace. It was time to go. Gorseth Arberth first, and then the Circle, and then, finally, the missioning into her own mother's womb.

She took a deep breath and signaled to the boatman.

A second chance with her mother and her father. It was not Arddu, but it was enough.